About the author

David Fuller is an FA-qualified football coach and currently coaches a youth football team in Brighton. He has worked as a journalist for over ten years, during which time he has written for numerous publications on a variety of different subjects. David lives in Newhaven, East Sussex with his wife, two sons and cat Merry.

Other books by David Fuller

Alfie Jones and a Test of Character
Alfie Jones and the Missing Link
Alfie Jones and an Uncertain Future
Alfie Jones and the Big Decision

To Isla

RDF Publishing
3 Courtlands Mews, Church Hill, Newhaven,
East Sussex,
BN9 9LU

Alfie Jones and a Change of Fortune
A RDF Publishing book

First published in Great Britain by RDF Publishing in 2011
This version published 2016
Printed and bound in Great Britain by Clays Ltd,
St Ives plc
5 2 4 3 1

Text copyright © David Fuller
Images courtesy of Rob Smyth
(http://www.robsmythart.com)

David Fuller asserts the moral right to
be identified as the author of this work

ISBN 978-0-9570339-0-0

For more exclusive Alfie Jones content, visit:
www.alfie-jones.co.uk

ALFIE JONES AND A CHANGE OF FORTUNE

DAVID FULLER

Illustrated by
Rob Smyth

www.alfie-jones.co.uk

Chapter one

Alfie Jones was cold, wet and miserable.

Earlier that morning Alfie had arrived at the Kingsway Recreation Ground, home of the Kingsway Colts under 9s football team, confident that today would be the day he would score his first ever goal for the Colts.

However, for the third Sunday in a row Alfie had been told by the team's new coach, Keith Johnson, that he was going to be a substitute. Again.

There were now only five minutes of the match left. The Colts were drawing 1-1 with Deansview Juniors. With so little time left, Alfie was starting to doubt whether he would get to play at all this week.

1

This would be the first time that Alfie had not played any part in a match. In the Colts' previous two games he'd got on the pitch for at least the last ten minutes in each. What's more, when he had been given the chance, he had not played at all badly.

Just last week he had set up a goal for his best friend and the team's star player, Billy Morris, and then managed to clear a shot off the goal-line in the last minute to help the Colts beat Ashgate Athletic 3-2.

'What more could I have done to get into the team?' Alfie now wondered silently to himself.

As rain continued to fall, Alfie was sitting on a bag full of footballs, daydreaming. His elbows dug into his knees and his head rested on his hands. His usually curly blond hair was so wet that it looked as though it had been superglued flat against his head, and his long fringe almost totally covered his blue eyes.

Usually, Alfie always wanted his team to win, even when he was a sub.

Today, however, he was not so sure. In fact, if he was being totally honest, Alfie would not have minded too much if the Colts were to let a goal in. That way he could play the role of super sub and score two quick goals to help Kingsway win the game.

Alfie was just thinking about how he would score the winning goal with a shot blasted so hard that the ball would rip right through the back of the net, when he heard his name being called.

"Alfie. Alfie Jones."

It took Alfie a second or two to realise that the voice belonged to Keith.

'Finally', Alfie thought to himself, 'I am going to get to play for a bit after all'.

But no sooner had Alfie stood up and started pulling at the zip on his soaking wet, blue Kingsway Colts tracksuit top, were his dreams of getting to be a super sub shattered.

"Don't sit on the balls, Jones," shouted Keith. "You'll make them all go egg shaped. Yes that's it; sit down on the floor. But watch out for that big... puddle."

The warning came a second too late. Alfie had already sat down right in the middle of a huge muddy puddle that had formed next to where he had been sitting.

Alfie pulled his knees into his body and started to rock gently to and fro.

He was on the brink of tears but he wouldn't let himself cry. Not yet. Not in front of his friends and all of the parents who were watching the game from the sidelines.

'If only Jimmy Grimshaw was still the team's coach,' Alfie thought to himself. 'Then I wouldn't be sub all of the time.'

Until recently, Jimmy Grimshaw had been the Kingsway Colts under 9s coach.

When Jimmy was in charge every boy and girl in the team got the chance to play in a different outfield position. And they all took turns at being substitute. Alfie loved playing in all the different outfield positions, especially striker, although he hated being a goalkeeper – "it's just sooo boring," he often moaned to Billy.

Jimmy had been coaching the Colts for many, many years – "my dad said at least since the dinosaurs were living," Billy had once told Alfie – but at the end of October Jimmy had become ill and been urged by his doctor to quit coaching.

Keith Johnson had replaced Jimmy as the team's coach.

Keith had only moved to Kingsway that summer along with his son, Jasper, who was the same age as Alfie.

But, unlike Alfie, Jasper was not very popular with his teammates.

4

On his first day at Kingsway Junior School, Jasper had boasted to everybody in the playground about how he was a much better footballer than anyone else at the school. The truth, though, was that he wasn't actually that good.

Jasper had joined the Kingsway Colts at the beginning of the season, much to the dismay of most of the team.

Once, when Jimmy told Jasper that it was his turn to be a substitute, Jasper became really angry and kicked a nearby water bottle as hard as he could.

The bottle narrowly missed hitting Chloe Reed, the Colts' only female player, square in the face.

When Keith took over as the Colts' coach, he immediately made his son the team's captain. He also said that, if he wanted to, Jasper could take penalties, free kicks and throw-ins.

"Jasper's much bigger and stronger than any of you lot," Keith had explained. "So he'll be able to kick the ball harder and throw it further."

This was indeed true. For a boy of his age, Jasper was simply huge. Unfortunately, because he was so big, this seemed to make him think that he could bully his teammates, especially Alfie who

5

was one of the smallest boys in his school year and also one of the shyest.

Back on the pitch the game was nearly over. Jasper had the ball at his feet. "Shoot son," shouted Keith. "There's only a few seconds left."

Jasper swung his right foot at the ball and kicked it as hard as he possibly could.

However, far from going straight, like it was supposed to, the ball instead flew right up into the air, just like a balloon does when you kick it. It was a truly terrible shot.

Fortunately, Billy had somehow guessed exactly where the ball was going to land and reached it before any of the Deansview defenders even had time to move. Billy controlled the ball perfectly with his chest and, without letting it bounce, volleyed the ball past the opposition goalkeeper and into the net. It was a goal that a professional footballer would have been proud of.

"Yeesss," exclaimed Keith excitedly. "Great pass Jasper. He couldn't miss."

Keith turned to look at Alfie. "Did you see that, Jones?" he asked with an unpleasant sneer spreading across his round, red face. "If you could pass a ball

6

like that then you wouldn't be sitting in a muddy puddle with a wet bum."

Alfie wanted to cry again. He knew that he was just as good a footballer as Jasper. He could keep the ball in the air without it bouncing using only his feet and knees six times nearly every time he tried – eight was his all-time record. He had only ever seen Jasper manage to do two keepy-ups, although the bigger boy told everyone he could do nine.

No one argued with Jasper, though. No one was big enough. Or brave enough.

Shortly after Billy had scored his wonder goal, the referee blew his whistle to signal the end of the match. All the Kingsway Colts players punched the air to celebrate their 2-1 victory before going off to shake hands with the defeated Deansview players.

All, that is, apart from Alfie, who just continued to sit in the muddy puddle looking increasingly glum.

After a few moments, Billy noticed that Alfie was still sitting all by himself. He looked very upset. Billy wandered over to his friend.

"What you sitting in that muddy puddle for, Alf?" asked a clearly confused Billy.

"Just am," Alfie answered, desperately

trying to stop his voice from croaking in the way it did when he was just about to cry.

"It's not fair that Keith made you sub again," said Billy, having realised why his friend was looking so down.

"Not bothered," Alfie glumly replied.

"Well…" said Billy, unsure of what he could say next to make Alfie feel any better. "… at least you're going to the funfair with your Mum and Dad this afternoon."

"Great," said Alfie, sounding even more miserable than he had before.

Just then, Billy's Dad walked over to the two boys. Mr Morris usually took both Billy and Alfie to football as Alfie's parents didn't really like the game and so tended to take his sister, Megan, to ballet on Sundays instead.

"Are you two nearly ready to get going?" asked Mr Morris. "Are you okay, Alfie? It's really not fair that Keith doesn't give you a fair chance. All of the parents were saying so. It's just not the same since Jimmy left. If things continue like this, we'll probably look for a new team next season and… Alfie?"

"Yeah?"

"Why are you sitting in a puddle?"

"He just is, Dad," answered Billy, fearing his friend was about to burst into tears.

With a big squelch, Alfie stood up. The back of his shorts were totally covered in thick, sludgy mud.

"I think we'll have to take those shorts off before you get in the car," said Mr Morris. "I'm not sure I'd ever have a clean car seat again if you sat in there with those on. You look muddier than a particularly unclean swamp monster!"

Alfie smiled. It wasn't a big smile but nevertheless it was the first smile that he had managed since being told he would be a sub earlier that morning.

As Mr Morris and the two children walked over to the car, they passed by Keith and Jasper. "How come you're muddier than me and didn't even play?" Jasper asked in a mocking tone of voice. "Were you splashing about in puddles like a little baby? I bet you wish you were as good at football as me, then you could actually play instead of just watch. Oh well, not everyone can be as good as me."

Mr Morris was about to tell Jasper to stop being so horrible and point out that, actually, he wasn't better than any of the other players, but Keith had already started to lead Jasper away towards their own car. Both father and son were laughing out loud.

Alfie clambered into the back seat of Mr Morris's car and finally started to cry.

Chapter two

Alfie didn't speak once during the
15-minute drive to his Mum and Dad's
house.

At first, Billy and Mr Morris had tried
to talk to him but Alfie ignored them. He
just stared out of the window, desperate
to be left alone.

After a few failed attempts to start a
conversation, Billy and his father gave up
trying and for the remaining ten minutes
of the journey nobody said a single word.

Once they had parked outside his house,
Alfie got out of the car, grunted a barely
audible thank you to Mr Morris, waved
a half-hearted goodbye to Billy and then

11

trudged slowly down the garden path to his front door.

The door was open before Alfie even had a chance to ring the bell.

"Hello love. How did you get on?" Alfie's Mum asked him in her usual cheerful manner. "Your sister won her ballet competition. She was just brilliant. So graceful. So..."

Alfie didn't answer his Mum. Nor did he wait to hear any more about how great his sister was at ballet. He brushed right past her without saying a word, then ran up the stairs and went straight into his bedroom, slamming the door shut behind him.

The inside of Alfie's bedroom was like a shrine to football. All four walls were covered by posters of his favourite players. He had got most of the posters free in the various football magazines which were stacked in unsteady piles at the foot of his bed. Player cards were also scattered all over the floor. There were so many cards and magazines on his bedroom floor that it was almost impossible to see any of the blue and white carpet that had been laid just a few weeks earlier.

Unlike many of his friends, Alfie didn't

support a particular team. He tended to like individual players instead, especially ones that scored lots of goals and played for England.

Twenty minutes after Alfie had slammed his bedroom door shut, he heard footsteps in the hallway, quickly followed by three knocks on his door. 'Now, I'm in trouble,' he thought to himself. 'I'm sure to get told off for slamming my door so hard.'

Following the final knock, the door opened almost immediately and Alfie's Dad walked into the room. Like Alfie, Mr Jones had blond curly hair. He was also quite short and very skinny in build. However, while Alfie had blue eyes, like his mother, his Dad's eyes were more of a greeny-grey colour.

Funnily enough, Megan had greeny-grey eyes like their Dad, but the same colour and type of hair as their Mum – brown and straight.

Mr Jones walked slowly over to the bed – which was covered by an England Three Lions duvet – on which Alfie was sitting reading an old copy of one of his magazines.

Having nearly tripped three times over one of the piles of magazines on the floor,

Mr Jones decided it would be safer to sit on the bed to talk to his son.

"All right, Alf?" Mr Jones asked tenderly.

Alfie nodded, sullenly, still fearing he was in trouble.

"Billy's Dad told us about what happened this morning. He said that you cried when you got in his car. Your mother and I have been talking. We think that if playing football is going to make you so upset, then maybe you shouldn't play for the Colts any more."

Alfie's expression changed for the first time in nearly an hour. Instead of looking miserable he just looked shocked. And then angry.

"Is, is this because I slammed my door?" Alfie stammered in response. Tears had started to form in the corner of his eyes.

"No. No of course not. It's because we don't want you to feel upset when you play football."

"But not playing football for the Colts would make me even more upset. All I want to do is play football."

"But that's the point, Alf. You're not playing football at the moment. Not since old Mr Grimshaw got ill. You're always a sub and…"

"But I won't always be a sub," Alfie interrupted. "I can get better if I practice lots and lots. Then I can play every week and score loads of goals. Just like Billy."

"But Billy's Dad also said that he thought you were being bullied by one of the boys. Jasper Johnson I think he said the boy's name was?"

Hearing his Dad say the name "Jasper Johnson" brought a brief flash of anger to Alfie's eyes. He was sure that it was Jasper's fault he wasn't being picked for the team. For some reason, Jasper didn't like him and Alfie was certain that this was the reason why Keith was not giving him a fair chance.

"Not bothered," Alfie said for the second time that day. Once again, though, it was very obvious that he was bothered.

"Look, we're not saying you have to give up football altogether," Mr Jones pressed on, knowing that to challenge his son about being bullied would only cause Alfie to go silent, just as he had in the back of Mr Morris's car. "We're just saying that maybe you could play for a different team. There are a few others close by and there was an advert in the local paper saying that Ashgate Athletic under 9s needs new players. I'm sure we could arrange something around your sister's ballet so that you could play for them instead."

"But Billy plays for the Colts," Alfie shouted. "I want to play for the same team as Billy. He's my best friend."

"Well, according to Mr Morris, Billy might leave next season to play for someone else anyway. It doesn't sound like he's very keen on this Jasper boy, either."

"But that's next season. I want to play for the same team as Billy now," said Alfie, almost pleading with his Dad to let him stay.

Realising that Alfie would be even more upset if he made him leave the Colts straight away, Mr Jones decided to offer his son a compromise. "Okay, how about this?" he began. "We'll let you stay with the Colts until Christmas. But if you're still sub all the time between now and then, then in January you can either look for a new team or maybe even give up playing football for a while."

Alfie took a minute or so to think about this.

On the one hand, there was no way he was going to stop playing football. He could go and play for Ashgate Athletic, but that would mean playing for a different team to Billy. However, while this wouldn't be ideal, it sure would be better than not playing at all or being a sub every week.

"Deal," Alfie agreed, nodding and holding his palm up so his Dad could high-five him. "But I'm not giving up football. If I can't get into the Colts team by Christmas then I'll play for Ashgate instead."

In truth, Mr Jones would have preferred Alfie to give up football. Without Mr Morris taking his son to the games, it would be difficult to get Megan to ballet on time every Sunday. Alfie's Dad didn't really like football and couldn't understand why his son was so passionate about the game. But he knew that football made Alfie happy (usually) and that was what he wanted his son to be. More than anything else in the world.

"Deal," said Dad high-fiving Alfie. "Now hurry up and get changed. We're going to the fun-fair this afternoon, remember?"

Alfie hadn't remembered. He really didn't feel like going. He was still in a bad mood from that morning's disappointment. "Do I have to go?" Alfie asked, poking his bottom lip over his top one. He always did this when he was sulking.

"Yes," said his Dad as he stood up and started to make his way to the door, being far more careful to avoid the piles of magazines strewn across the floor this time. "And Alfie, one more question."

"Yes Dad?"

"Just what did you do to your football shorts this morning? It looks like you've been living in a swamp for the past month."

With that Mr Jones walked out of the room and shut the door behind him, leaving Alfie to get changed for the fun-fair. He was still desperate not to go but knew there was no way he would be able to get out of it.

What Alfie didn't know, however, was that that very afternoon he would meet someone who would change the course of his life forever.

Chapter three

It had continued raining all afternoon.
While this had not dampened the spirits
of Megan or Mr and Mrs Jones – all of
whom were having a great time at the
fun-fair – Alfie's mood had not improved
one bit since the morning.

  In fact, Alfie was by now feeling so glum
that he had only managed to eat half of
his big bag of candy floss.

  Even more unusually, he hadn't once
tried to barge into his younger sister
while they were on the dodgems.
Crashing into Megan's bumper car was
usually a source of great amusement
to Alfie. He would simply delight in

crashing his dodgem car into his sister's as hard and fast as he possibly could – although he always told his parents that the collisions were an accident. Not that they ever believed him.

Finally, at least as far as Alfie was concerned, it was almost time to leave the fun-fair. His parents had promised him that once Megan had finished her fourth ride on the merry-go-round they would be ready to head home.

Alfie couldn't wait to get back to his bedroom and open the three packets of football cards that his Mum and Dad had bought him on the way to the fun-fair.

He was just leaning against some railings by the merry-go-round, half watching his Dad and sister swing past on their plastic horses, half day-dreaming about his football cards, when he thought he heard a female voice quietly calling his name.

"Did you call me?" Alfie asked his Mum, who was standing next to him.

"No darling," replied Mrs Jones, whilst waving frantically at Megan and Mr Jones as they swung past her for the umpteenth time.

Alfie scratched his head. He was certain a woman had called his name. Other than his Mum and Megan, though, he didn't know any other women at the fair. He must have been mistaken.

However, just seconds later, Alfie heard his name being called again. This time the voice was much louder and clearer.

"Alfie Jones. Alfie Jones. Come here Alfie Jones."

It sounded like the words were coming from behind him. But when Alfie spun around to look, the only thing he could see was a small green tent with a blackboard outside it. Written on the blackboard in chalk were the words 'Madam Zola, Fortune Teller. Learn your future here.'

'That's strange,' Alfie thought to himself. 'I don't remember seeing a fortune teller here earlier.'

He was just about to turn back round when something suddenly caught his eye. More words had started to appear on the blackboard.

Now underneath the line 'Learn your future here.' Alfie could clearly see his name scrawled in the same chalk writing followed by 'come inside... Now!'

Alfie tugged hard on his Mum's sleeve. "Mum. Look at that blackboard. Quick."

Mrs Jones turned round almost

instantly. "What is it darling?"

"Look at that blackboard over there?" Alfie almost shouted, pointing frantically towards the tent.

"What about it, sweetie? It's just a fortune teller's tent. Hmmm. That's weird. I don't remember seeing it there earlier. Oh well, I suppose wasn't looking for it."

"But what about what it says on that blackboard. Why's my name written on it? I... I don't understand."

Mrs Jones narrowed here eyes and stared at the board. Her eyesight wasn't great, especially as she often refused to wear her glasses, so she really had to concentrate hard to read things from long distances.

After a brief pause she said, "Your name's not on it darling. It just says 'Madam Zola, Fortune Teller. Learn your future here.' I think you must be tired. It's okay; we'll be going home soon." With that she turned back to face the merry-go-round.

Alfie, however, could not take his eyes off of the board. There was no question that his name was written on the board along with instructions for him to go inside.

By the time the merry-go-round ride had finished, and Megan and Mr Jones had rejoined them by the railings, Alfie was still staring intently at the board.

Mr Jones tapped Alfie on the shoulder. "Ready to go then, Alf?"

"Can I go and see that fortune teller first?" Alfie replied, still without so much as taking his eyes off the blackboard.

"But I thought you wanted to go home?"

"Well now I want to stay. Oh go on," Alfie pleaded, finally looking at his Dad and clasping his hands together. "Megan's been on that merry-go-round like a hundred times. I just want to do this one thing. Please."

"Well, I've got no idea why you want to see a fortune teller, but I suppose it's not a problem. I didn't even know there was one here actually. Never mind. Would you like me or your Mum to go in with you?"

"No, that's fine," said Alfie, who had already started running towards the tent. "I want to go in by myself."

As he neared the opening of the tent, Alfie looked at the blackboard one final time. More chalk writing had appeared on it, even though nobody had been near the tent the entire time he had been looking at it.

The board now read: 'Madam Zola, Fortune Teller. Learn your future here. Alfie Jones, come inside... Now! Important news awaits."

Alfie's heart was beating as fast as it had ever done before. How did the fortune teller know his name and just what was it she wanted to tell him?

Alfie couldn't wait to find out.

Chapter four

Although the fortune teller's tent may
have looked small from the outside,
inside it was absolutely huge – about the
size of a full-sized football pitch in length
and as big as a house in height.

There were loads of what looked to
Alfie like wind-chimes hanging from the
ceiling, and at the far end of the tent
there was a table with a crystal ball on it.

Other than that the tent was completely
empty. Madam Zola was nowhere to be
seen.

Alfie didn't know what to do next.

Maybe his Mum had been right. Maybe
he had just been seeing and hearing

things. After all, he was always being told by his school teachers that he had an overactive imagination.

"Hello. Hello. Is there anybody here?" Alfie called out, cautiously.

There was no answer.

Alfie walked slowly over to the table and started to closely examine the crystal ball. In truth, the ball didn't look crystal at all. It looked more like it was made of glass. Just how anyone was supposed to see into the future by staring into a glass ball, Alfie wasn't entirely sure.

After looking at the ball for a while, and seeing nothing, Alfie got on to his hands and knees to have a good look under the table to see if he could see anything. There was still nothing to be found.

'Well that settles it,' Alfie thought to himself. 'There's no one here so nobody can have been calling me and my name can't have been written on the blackboard outside the tent. I really must have just imagined it all!'

Feeling more than a little disappointed, Alfie decided that there was nothing left for him to do but to leave the fortune teller's tent and find his parents and sister so they could all finally go home.

He began to plod miserably towards the

exit, but had got no more than halfway there when one of the wind-chimes began to chime. 'There must be a draught somewhere,' Alfie reasoned to himself.

All of a sudden, though, another wind chime began making a noise. Then another. And then another.

Within seconds, all of the wind chimes had started chiming. The noise was deafening.

Alfie started to panic. Although he didn't like to admit to ever being scared, he couldn't deny that at that very moment he was petrified.

He started sprinting towards the tent's exit when, all at once, every single one of the wind chimes stopped making a noise.

There was a second of absolute silence before Alfie heard someone call his name. It was the same voice that had been calling him when he'd been standing outside by the merry-go-round.

The voice was coming from the direction of the table behind him, but when Alfie spun around he could no longer see the table. All he could see was thick, swirling smoke.

He was about to turn and run again, when through the smoke he caught a glimpse of something. It was the shape of

a person and they were walking towards
him. Then he clearly heard someone
coughing and spluttering. A lot.

Alfie was rooted to the spot, frozen by
fear.

Chapter five

Within seconds, the mysterious figure
had fully emerged from the smoke and
was now clearly visible to Alfie.

"Alfie. Alfie Jones. That is you, isn't it?"
the person called out, before bursting into
another fit of coughs.

Alfie said nothing. He couldn't speak.
He was too scared.

"Bloomin' smoke. Gets me like this
every time," the person, who by now Alfie
had worked out to be the woman that
had been calling him, said to nobody in
particular.

The woman continued to cough for a
while longer before eventually managing

to clear her throat enough to be able to speak some more. "Don't be scared, Alfie. I'm Madam Zola." The fortune teller coughed again. "Sorry for not being here just now when you came in. I was... er... I was... elsewhere."

Alfie wanted to ask her where exactly she had been. He'd looked everywhere in the tent without seeing her, and it wasn't like there were many places to hide in there. But he still could not bring himself to speak. He just stood staring at her, unsure of what he should do next.

Madam Zola looked old. Really old. She had long grey hair which was partly covered by something resembling a purple tea-towel. At first Alfie thought that she looked a bit like a witch – she had a huge crooked nose and a long thin face – but after examining her for a bit longer he decided that she seemed too kind looking to be a witch. She had twinkly brown eyes and a very friendly smile. She wore a long green and purple gown which completely covered her feet and when she walked towards Alfie he thought it looked as though she was floating towards him.

"Its okay, Alfie. There's no need to be scared. I just need to talk to you. I've got

some very exciting news." Madam Zola's
voice was soft and welcoming. Alfie was
slowly starting to become less frightened
of the mysterious fortune teller.

"Will you come and sit with me at the
table for a moment?" the old woman
asked, gesturing towards the table with
the crystal ball on it. The smoke had by
now completely disappeared.

Alfie thought for a bit, then nodded and
followed Madam Zola to the table.

Once they were both sitting on opposite
sides of the table, Madam Zola began to
speak. Both of her hands were placed on
the crystal/glass ball. Alfie couldn't help

but notice that she had very long, thin fingers.

"Now Alfie, I understand you love football. Is that right?" she asked.

Alfie nodded once again. He hadn't been that impressed by the fortune teller's deduction.

He was wearing an England football tracksuit and he was a nine-year-old boy. Of course he loved football.

"And am I right in thinking that you haven't been getting in the Kingsway Colts under 9s team recently? That you've only been a substitute?"

This made Alfie sit up straight. His blue eyes opened wide and he looked at the fortune teller in wonderment. How could she possibly know that? The fortune teller now had his full attention.

"Yes. That's right," Alfie answered. It was the first time he had spoken since Madam Zola had appeared and his words came out slowly. "How. How. How..."

"How do I know this?" Madam Zola continued, finishing the question that Alfie had clearly been struggling to ask. "I know everything about you, Alfie. I know that you've got a sister called Megan; a best friend called Billy Morris and that there's a boy on your team called

Jasper Johnson who you really don't get on with. Am I correct?"

Alfie didn't say anything. Once again he found himself unable to speak. But this time it was not fear that had forced him into silence – it was amazement. He wanted to hear what else the fortune teller had to say.

"You're impressed aren't you? I can always tell when people are. It's a gift I have. Well, one of them. I have many gifts as you will find out in time. Anyway, this is what I have to tell you..."

The old lady cleared her throat, an action which brought on yet another long bout of coughing and spluttering. "Sorry about that. Now, where were we? Oh yes, that's right. I know that your Dad has told you that you can't continue playing for the Colts if you can't get into the team by Christmas. But you cannot allow this to happen! You must get into the team and you must stay with the Colts. It's very important that you do, for your own sake."

"Wh. Why?" Alfie had to force the word out. He could not understand how the fortune teller knew so much about him. He'd only had the conversation about possibly having to leave the Colts with his Dad earlier that afternoon. How could she have known about it?

"Because if you don't you won't be able to fulfil your destiny."

"I don't understand. What destiny?"

"That you'll grow up to be the one thing that you want to be more than anything else in the world."

"You mean..."

"That's right, Alfie Jones. Stay with the Colts and one day you will be a professional footballer!"

Chapter six

During the following week, Alfie spent more time practising football than he had ever done before.

He took his own ball with him to school so that he could practice keepy-ups during break times. In the evenings, he spent hours in his bedroom bouncing a ball against a wall and then trying to head or volley the rebound into a goal that he had made on his bed. In the end his Mum and Dad had told him to stop doing this as the thud the ball made when it hit the wall was keeping Megan awake. All the more reason to do it, Alfie had thought to himself.

He had not told any of his friends about what Madam Zola had said to him. In fact, when they asked him whether he'd enjoyed the fun-fair he didn't mention anything about having seen a fortune teller. Most of them probably wouldn't believe him anyway. Even Billy might think he was being a bit silly, while Jasper would definitely take the mickey out of him – even more than he did already.

He had told his Mum and Dad, however, and while they were pleased to see their son happy again, they strongly advised Alfie not to get too carried away by what the fortune teller had told him. "Fortune tellers don't always get everything right, Alf. Try not to get your hopes up too much," Mr Jones warned him.

But Alfie was convinced that Madam Zola was right about this. He was sure she had special powers – far more special than those most fortune tellers possess. How else could she have known so much about him? How else could she have just appeared from nowhere inside the tent? How else could a message to him have suddenly appeared on the blackboard without anybody being around to write it?

He was going to be a professional footballer one day, he just knew he was.

In order for that to happen, though, Alfie first had to start playing regularly for the Colts. If he couldn't get into the team by Christmas he knew his Dad was going to make him join Ashgate Athletic.

He had tried telling his parents that he had to stay at the Colts no matter what, otherwise his destiny would not come true. They wouldn't listen. As far as Alfie's Dad was concerned they had made a deal and they were going to stick to it.

There were only three games left before Christmas, so Alfie was fast running out of time to win back his place in the team. He knew that he would have to work really hard to impress Keith and be picked, but he was determined to do all he could to make sure it happened.

By the following Saturday morning's training session it was clear for all to see just how hard Alfie had been practising. His passing was better than it had ever been before, his ball control was much improved and he even scored a hat-trick in the mini-match that the Colts played to finish every practice.

The third of these goals was particularly satisfying as Jasper had been the opposition's goalkeeper. Alfie had taken the ball round him with ease before scoring, making the coach's son look a little foolish in the process.

Jasper was not impressed one bit. He blamed everyone on his team except for himself for letting "the little muppet score." Keith agreed with his son, saying that the defence had "made it far too easy for Alfie" and left Jasper "helpless."

At the end of the session, Billy and Chloe, both of whom had also been on the opposite team to Alfie during the match, went to congratulate their friend on how well he had played.

"Wow, Alfie, you were great today. I've never seen you play so well," enthused Billy.

"Yeah, there's no way Keith won't pick you for the match against Brook Wanderers tomorrow after that performance," added Chloe.

Just then, Jasper came strolling over to them. For the slightest moment, Alfie thought that even Jasper was going to tell him how well he had played.

He was wrong.

"You just got lucky today, muppet," snarled the larger boy. "You'll still be sub tomorrow."

Unbelievably Jasper was right –
something that didn't happen all that
often. When Keith read out the team
the following morning, Alfie was still not
named among the starters.

He could not believe it. Once again he
would be spending a Sunday morning
sitting on the side of a pitch watching his
friends play football.

There was nothing more that he could
possibly have done to be picked. There
simply weren't enough hours in the day to
practice any more than he had spent that
past week doing – unless he went without
sleep or refused to do his homework.
He rightly guessed that neither of these
options would be allowed by his Mum and
Dad.

Some of the watching parents, including
Billy's Dad, walked up to Alfie to say they
thought it was extremely unfair that he
was sub again.

It didn't make him feel any better,
though. In fact, Alfie felt sick. Not only
was he extremely upset about being a
sub again, but he was now convinced
there was no way he would be able to get
into the team by Christmas. A move to
Ashgate Athletic was almost certain.

Alfie's destiny would not come true.

Chapter seven

The match against Brook Wanderers started terribly for the Colts.

Most of the team had spent the first ten minutes of the match still angry about Keith's decision to make Alfie sub again and hadn't been able to motivate themselves properly.

Brook had taken full advantage and stormed into a two goal lead.

Keith was not impressed by his team's slow start to the game. "What's up with you lot today?" he bellowed from the sideline. "It's only Jasper who's trying out there!"

This was not strictly untrue. Jasper,

who was not in the slightest bit bothered by Alfie's fate, was indeed working harder than the rest of his teammates. However, as usual, the moment Jasper got the ball he simply just toe punted it forward as hard as he could, leading to the ball either going off the field for a throw in or goal kick to the other team.

"If only any of you lot were as good as Jasper then we wouldn't be in this mess," Keith yelled, much to the dismay of the other Colts players and the watching parents.

Billy, who had been standing near the sideline where Keith was, could not believe what his coach was saying. 'So he thinks Jasper's better than me, does he?' Billy thought to himself. 'Well, we'll soon see about that.'

Moments later, Billy received the ball to his feet for the first time in the match and set off on one of his trademark mazy dribbles up the pitch. He left three Brook players trailing in his wake as he made his way speedily towards the opposition's penalty area.

However, the final Brook defender had not proved so easy for Billy to get past and had managed to force him out wide. This had given the beaten defenders enough time to recover and they were now all quickly closing in on the Colts' star player.

There was no other option but for Billy to pass to a teammate. Unfortunately, he had run so fast that none of the other Colts players had been able to keep up with him. The only player who was in a good position to pass to was Jasper, who had not bothered to run back following the Colts' previous attack. 'Oh well,' thought Billy, 'I'll pass to Jasper. He is in the best position, after all.'

Billy's pass was inch perfect. The ball rolled straight along the floor and landed right at Jasper's feet. The Colts' captain was totally unmarked and only five yards away from the goal. He had so much time to do whatever he wanted with the ball that he could have had a glass of orange juice if he'd wanted one and still been able to have a free shot at goal.

However, instead of taking his time, Jasper just smashed the ball as hard as he could, sending it flying high over the crossbar and into a duck pond situated quite a long way behind the goal.

Jasper glared hard at Billy. "What sort of a pass was that? You hit it far too hard. And the pitch is really uneven. And...

And... Well... You're just rubbish!"

Billy was about to angrily respond and point out a few of his captain's own failings when to his, and almost everyone else's, surprise, Keith also started to blame him.

"Come on Billy," shouted Keith, who was so angry that he had gone even redder in the face than usual. "There's no point doing all those flashy skills if you can't even make a simple pass."

The manager then turned to Alfie. "Come on then, Jones. Up you get. Go and get the ball out of the pond. We'll have to make do with one of the spare ones until you get back so hurry up."

As Billy furiously made his way back into his position, shaking his head and looking at his Dad, who also looked really angry, Alfie walked dejectedly towards the duck pond.

The ball was right over the other side of the pond, which meant he would have to cross at the rickety old footbridge some 30 yards away in order to get to it. Thankfully, the ball was near the edge of the pond, so at least he would not have to get wet in order to reach it.

When Alfie got to the bridge he heard some cheering coming from the pitch.

He looked round only to see that Brook had scored again. The Colts were losing 3-0 and it wasn't even half-time yet. "I bet I still won't get on," he murmured unhappily to himself.

Having retrieved the ball from the pond, Alfie was just about to walk back across the bridge when he thought he saw something move in a nearby bush. Deciding that there was no real need to hurry back to the pitch as there wasn't much chance of him playing anyway, he went to look at what it was that had caught his eye.

To his amazement, there was a black cat playing in the middle of the bush. It was chasing a leaf. The cat saw Alfie and walked towards him immediately. It rubbed against Alfie's legs and the boy in turn tickled the cat's chin. The cat responded by purring loudly. Alfie loved cats but his Mum and Dad wouldn't let him have one as Megan was allergic to their fur.

Seconds later, Alfie heard a faint rattling noise from somewhere in the distance. It sounded like someone was shaking a box of cat biscuits. The cat responded to the noise instantly and began running as fast as it could towards the sound of the rattle. Alfie watched the cat for a moment as it ran towards an old woman, who was indeed standing there shaking a box of cat biscuits, and then turned back towards the direction of the pitch.

'I suppose I should get back with the ball,' Alfie thought to himself. 'Keith will probably blame that last goal on me because we weren't using the proper match ball or something equally stupid.'

Alfie had put one foot on the bridge before he suddenly stopped in his tracks. There was something familiar about the person who had been holding the cat biscuit box. He turned to look to see if the old woman was still there. She was.

Alfie could not believe his eyes. Although she was standing quite a long way away, he recognised her instantly. The green and purple gown she was wearing was unmistakable. It was Madam Zola.

The fortune teller held a hand up and waved to Alfie. After a moment of hesitation, Alfie responded with a wave of his own.

He was about to start walking towards the old woman when he heard Keith shouting his name. The call sounded urgent. He took a quick look over his shoulder. Keith was signalling frantically at Alfie and yelling for him to get back over to the pitch "RIGHT THIS MINUTE!"

'They must have lost all the spare balls,' Alfie reasoned to himself. 'I'd better get back or I'll never stand a chance of getting a game.'

The boy turned to wave goodbye to Madam Zola, but the fortune teller was already gone. So too was the cat.

Alfie strained his eyes, but all he could see was someone walking a dog. He smiled ruefully to himself. "Typical. She's disappeared," he said aloud, and then ran back to the pitch.

When he got there it turned out that it wasn't the ball that Keith needed. It was Alfie.

The players from both teams were all standing in a huddle along with the referee and Keith. They were crowded around Des Grey, who was playing in midfield for the Colts. He was lying on the ground.

"What happened?" asked Alfie as he approached the huddle.

"Des has hurt himself," Chloe replied. "Nobody saw what happened but Des says he twisted his left ankle as he was running."

"Owww," Des cried out, a grimace stretching right across his face. "It really, really hurts," he moaned. The young boy was clearly in a lot of pain. "I don't want to play anymore." There were tears rolling down Des's cheeks and it was obvious for all to see that he wouldn't be able to continue playing.

"You heard the boy, Jones," said Keith as he lifted Des off the ground and started to help the injured boy off the pitch. "He can't play on, so I suppose you'll have to play instead. Get that tracksuit off and get on. We're already 3-0 down and there's still five minutes until half-time. Try not to make things any worse."

Although this wasn't the way Alfie wanted to get a game – Des was one of his best friends – he also knew that this was the perfect chance to show Keith what he could do and force his way into the team for good.

He was sure that the next 25 minutes would prove vital in keeping his dream alive.

Chapter eight

The remaining five minutes of the half passed without any further incident.

Alfie had yet to touch the ball as he tried to adapt to the pace of the game. He always found it really hard to get involved in a match when he came on as sub, but today he was more determined than ever to make a positive impact.

Keith was still tending to the injured Des on the side of the pitch, so there was no one available to give the Colts a half-time team talk.

Jasper tried to take his Dad's place by telling his teammates to pass the ball to him and that he'd do the rest, but no one

48

was listening. The rest of the team were chatting among themselves – some were worried about Des's ankle, while others were plotting how they were going to recover from being three goals behind.

As the Colts walked back on to the pitch for the second half, Billy pulled Alfie to one side. "Just play like you did yesterday in training and you'll be fine," he said. "Don't listen to anything Jasper says. My Dad just told me to just ignore him and concentrate on my own game so that's what I'm going to do. You should try and do the same."

Alfie nodded. He had caught a glimpse at the look on Mr Morris's face when Keith had blamed Billy for Jasper's shocking shot at goal. His friend's Dad was clearly not happy, although he had said nothing to Keith about the incident.

The angry look on Mr Morris's face had reminded Alfie of his own Dad's expression the time he'd tied Megan's shoelaces together, causing her to fall over. She had grazed one side of her face quite badly and Alfie had been banned from playing football for two weeks and had all of his magazines and cards taken away from him. He had not done anything like that since.

'I wish Mr Morris could ban Keith from football,' Alfie thought to himself as he waited for the referee to blow his whistle to start the second half.

The first few minutes of the second half started in much the same way as the first half had, with Brook doing almost all of the attacking. With just over ten minutes of the game left, the score was still 3-0, but only thanks to three spectacular saves by Pranav Jamal, the Colts' goalkeeper.

While the Colts weren't playing well as a team, Alfie had himself managed to have a couple of neat touches. First he had produced a good first-time lay-off to Billy, who shot wide. Then he had played a defence splitting pass to Liam Walker who couldn't quite get to the ball before the Brook goalkeeper.

However, he still needed to be more involved. And he knew it.

Just then, the Colts got their first slice of luck in the match. A long, hopeful punt from a goal kick taken by Jasper – he insisted on taking them instead of Pranav as he could kick the ball much further – should have been easily dealt with by a Brook defender. However, as the unfortunate centre back went to kick the ball clear he slipped over and the ball ran straight through to Billy who had continued chasing after what had seemed to be a lost cause.

Once Billy was clear of the defence there was no chance that anybody would be able to catch him. The winger dribbled the ball right to the edge of the penalty area, waited for the Brook goalkeeper to come out of his goal, and then coolly slipped the ball past him to make it 3-1. The Colts were back in the game.

"What a pass," shouted Jasper, as he ran around the pitch with his arms raised in the air. "I am the greatest," he started singing loudly.

To look at him you would have thought that Jasper had just scored a hat-trick in the World Cup final, not toe punted a ball as hard as he could, and then relied on luck along with Billy's pace and skill, to get his team a goal.

Keith had looked up just in time to see Billy score and was beaming with pride at his son's part in the goal. "You are the greatest," the manager sang back to his son. Billy and Alfie, as Mr Morris had suggested, just ignored the antics of their team's coach and captain, and continued to concentrate on the game.

51

"Great goal, Billy," Alfie said, high fiving his buddy.

"Thanks. Your turn next," replied Billy.

Alfie hoped that his friend would be right.

***

The goal certainly gave the Colts' some extra belief in themselves and for the first time in the match they started to put the Wanderers' defence under constant pressure.

During the next five minutes, Kingsway came close to scoring twice. First a long-range shot from Liam led to the ball smacking against the crossbar, and then Chloe headed Billy's pin-point cross inches past the post.

Alfie was still working hard and playing quite well, but he knew he would need to do more than play just quite well in order to keep his place in the team.

"Keep going, Alfie," urged Billy, after Chloe's header had just missed the target. "Just concentrate on your game, like I said at half-time. We need all of our best players to play as well as they can."

Hearing Billy describe him as one of the team's best players seemed to give Alfie the extra confidence boost he needed.

From the Brook goal kick, which had resulted from Chloe's missed header, Alfie intercepted the goalkeeper's intended pass and controlled the ball on his chest. Then, instead of passing the ball to one of his teammates, which is what he had done every other time he'd had control of the football, he decided to take it up the field by himself.

He beat the first Brook defender by putting the ball through their legs. "Great nutmeg," he heard someone – he thought it was Mr Morris – shout from the sideline. He beat the second defender with another trick he'd been practising during the previous week. He dropped his left shoulder to make it look as if he was going to swerve to the left but at the last minute he went to the right, leaving the hapless defender on the floor, totally bamboozled by the small midfielder's sudden change of direction.

"Keep going Alfie," he heard most of the watching parents shout. Even Des was cheering him on, despite the pain he was so obviously in.

However, Alfie wasn't as fast as Billy and he knew he wouldn't have enough speed to make it into the penalty area without being caught. Although he was still quite a long way from goal Alfie shaped his body as if to shoot. He swung his left leg back as far as he could and then brought it forward quickly. Everyone held their breath. They looked towards the Brook goal to see if the ball would beat the goalkeeper.

But Alfie hadn't shot.

He'd managed to fool everybody – well, almost everybody.

Instead of smashing the ball as hard as he could, he had instead passed the ball to Liam, who was standing just six yards from goal. With everyone else expecting a shot the Colts striker was totally unmarked and Liam had the simple task of tapping the ball into the empty net.

It was a move that the two boys had spoken about trying during training the day before – and it had worked perfectly.

There was no time for celebrations, though. "Get the ball out of the goal, Liam," Alfie shouted to his friend. "There's still enough time to score another one."

The Kingsway Colts players had now forgotten all about Keith's unfair treatment of Alfie – and Des's injury. Each and every one of them was putting all their efforts into getting an unlikely draw from the match.

However, time was fast running out and Brook Wanderers were defending really well.

Alfie noticed the referee look at his watch. He knew they did this when it was nearly full-time. Billy had the ball near the right hand sideline but he was being tracked by two defenders and had nowhere to go. It was now or never for Alfie to make a real impact.

He made a clever run down the line. One the player who was marking him hadn't expected. "Pass Billy," called Alfie at the top of his voice.

Billy obliged and suddenly Alfie found himself in plenty of space on the edge of the penalty area. Without thinking, he shifted the ball onto his left foot – his preferred kicking foot – and took a shot at goal, aiming for the far corner of the net.

His foot connected with the ball perfectly. The Brook goalkeeper was helpless and could only stand and watch as the ball flew past him.

Alfie braced himself – the shot was going in. He was going to score. He was going to be the hero...

Except he wasn't.

The ball was just about to cross the goal line when Jasper came running in as fast as he could and, for no reason whatsoever, blasted the ball over the line from only inches away. It was 3-3.

"Whoo-hoo," a clearly delighted Jasper yelled at the top of his voice. He ran over to where his Dad and the parents of the Colts players were standing and slid on his knees in front of them. Keith was jumping up and down celebrating. None of the other parents were even clapping.

In his mind Jasper had expected to be mobbed by his teammates for scoring what he viewed as a heroic goal.

He was therefore hugely disappointed when no one joined him.

After a few seconds of kneeling on his own in front of the clearly unimpressed parents – other than his Dad, of course – Jasper looked behind him to see what had happened to his teammates. To his astonishment, they were celebrating with Alfie.

"What are you lot doing?" An obviously very annoyed Jasper shouted to them. "That was my goal. I scored. I'm the hero, not him. It wasn't even a good pass; I had to run miles to get there in time to score."

Everyone continued to ignore Jasper, which only served to make their captain even more furious. "What's wrong with you lot?" Jasper whined angrily. "I've set a goal up and scored one yet you'd still rather celebrate with that muppet. He's only playing because Des hurt himself. You're all idiots."

"They're all just jealous of you, son. Don't worry about it," Keith said quietly to Jasper so that only his son could hear him. "I know you're better than all of the others put together. They'll realise it as well one day."

There was hardly time for the match to restart before the referee blew his whistle to signal full-time. Most of the players from both teams shook hands with each other and it was widely agreed that, in the end, a draw was a fair result.

Jasper, however, hadn't shaken hands with anyone. He had stormed off the pitch as soon as the final whistle had sounded and gone to speak to his Dad about something.

Both father and son looked over to Alfie and started laughing – something both Alfie and Billy saw them doing.

"They look like they're up to something and it looks like it's got something to do with you," said Billy.

Alfie nodded. He totally agreed with his friend.

The only question was just what exactly did Keith and Jasper have in store for him?

Chapter nine

At school the following day, Alfie was treated like a hero by his teammates.

"My Dad said that you were easily the man of the match yesterday, even though you only played just over half the game," Billy told him at break time.

"My Mum said the same thing," said Liam, who was walking with them to the playground where they were going to play football in spite of the freezing cold weather. It was early December and it was now starting to get really chilly. Alfie's Dad had said it might even snow in time for Christmas.

When they got to the playground everyone wanted to have Alfie on their team. His impressive performance against Brook Wanderers had been the talk of the school that morning and suddenly Alfie found himself even more in demand than Billy was when it came to picking teams. Not that his best friend seemed to mind.

Even Jasper hadn't said anything nasty to Alfie that morning. There were no comments about him being rubbish at football and he hadn't even called him muppet once.

In fact, the larger boy had even smiled at Alfie and said good morning to him in a pleasant manner while they were queuing up to get into their classroom at the start of the day.

"Maybe he's not going to pick on you anymore," Chloe had said.

"Maybe," Alfie replied, although he didn't really believe for one second that this would be the case. He didn't trust Jasper as far as he could throw him, and given the considerable size difference between the two boys, Alfie doubted he could even lift the Colts' captain, let alone throw him.

Alfie was still full of confidence during

the break time match, and started trying even more skills that he'd been practising over the past week – most of which worked.

Billy even asked Alfie to show him one of the turns he'd been working on. Alfie had called the turn the 'whizzy-dizzy'. It basically involved running around the ball lots and lots of times until your opponent got so dizzy they couldn't concentrate anymore and you could then easily run past them with the ball.

The turn didn't work every time you tried it, and it could sometimes leave you feeling sick if you spun around once too often, but when it did work it did look really, really impressive.

"That's sooo cool," said Billy, as Alfie showed him what to do. "I'm going to practice that and try to use it in our game against Heath Hill United on Sunday."

While Alfie was flattered that his friend wanted to use the 'whizzy-dizzy' turn for himself, he hoped that Billy wouldn't get a chance to use it before he did. After all, he had invented the turn. It was only right that he should get to use it in a real match first.

Of course, that would mean he'd have to be picked to play – but given how well he'd played against Brook Wanderers he was sure that Keith wouldn't be able to ignore him this week.

The chances of Alfie being picked for the match against Heath Hill increased even more on Tuesday when Des turned up to school on crutches. He hadn't been in on Monday as the hospital had told him to completely rest his ankle for 24 hours.

"It's not broken, but it is really badly sprained," Des told his friends. "The doctor said I won't be able to play until early next year."

Although everyone expressed sympathy for Des, Alfie and his friends were all secretly thinking that this would mean that he would almost certainly start the match on Sunday.

By Saturday morning's training session, Alfie had continued practising hard during the week and had spent most break times impressing his school friends with new tricks that he'd come up with in his bedroom the night before.

Jasper hadn't been horrible to him all week, but something about the way he was acting still didn't feel right to Alfie. Something about the way he kept looking at him and smiling was making the smaller boy nervous.

Even Keith seemed to be more encouraging that usual towards Alfie during practice. This only made him feel more wary that something was not quite right. Billy felt the same, but neither of the boys could work out what it was Keith and Jasper were planning.

Despite his suspicions regarding what Keith and Jasper were up to, Alfie scored a hat-trick for the second week running during the mini-match. Even though the team he was on ended up losing the game 7-5, he was still extremely pleased with the way he had played.

There was no doubting the major improvements that Alfie had made to his game since his first meeting with Madam Zola almost two weeks earlier. While he acknowledged that some of these improvements were probably a result of the increased time he was spending practising, he felt that there was something more to it than just hard work.

It was almost as if Madam Zola was helping him get better in some way. Surely, Alfie reasoned, it couldn't have been a coincidence that he'd seen her again just seconds before Des had got injured, and he'd then gone on to play his best game ever.

What was she doing at Kingsway Recreation Ground anyway? And why did she have a cat with her? There certainly was something strange about that woman.

Alfie was thinking about all this while he was putting on his trainers – Mr Morris wouldn't let anybody into his car with muddy football boots on – when Keith wandered over to him.

"Hi Jones, I mean Alfie," Keith said. "I just wanted to let you know that you'll definitely be starting the game tomorrow." He smiled at Alfie and then walked off.

Alfie could see Jasper watching this conversation from a distance away. His smile exactly mirrored the one on his Dad's face.

"That's great news, Alfie," exclaimed Mr Morris, who had heard what Keith had told him. "You definitely deserve it."

But Alfie wasn't so sure that it was great news. Something about the way Keith and Jasper were smiling just didn't feel right.

Chapter ten

That afternoon all Alfie wanted to do
was spend some time alone in his room
reading football magazines and practising
some new tricks.

Even though he couldn't shake the
feeling that Keith and Jasper were up to
something, he was still delighted about
being told he would be starting the next
day's match. He couldn't wait to try out
his new skills in a real game. He was
determined to do the 'whizzy-dizzy' turn
before Billy got a chance to.

But it was the day of Megan's school's
Christmas fete and he'd already been told
by his Mum and Dad that, as they were

both going, he would have to go as well.

"Don't look so miserable, darling. Father Christmas will be there," his Mum assured him.

"Great," he replied grumpily.

However, although Alfie pretended he was too cool to care about Father Christmas – he knew that it wouldn't be the real one, just somebody dressed up pretending to be him – the truth was that he still got excited about seeing Santa. Especially as it meant he'd get a present – even though it was bound to be something he didn't really want.

Megan, on the other hand, did not bother to disguise her excitement about seeing Father Christmas. Alfie's sister loved him and she didn't care who knew it. She was bouncing up and down so much that you would have thought that she'd just drunk a whole bottle of Coca-Cola – something which always made her super hyperactive.

From the moment Mr Morris had dropped Alfie home from football practice, Megan had been pestering her brother to hurry up and get ready. This, of course, had only made Alfie even more determined to take his time getting bathed and changed. He loved winding his little sister up. It was his favourite hobby – after football.

Eventually, Mr Jones had to order Alfie to hurry up as Megan's constant whingeing about how long her older brother was taking to get ready had started to drive him round the bend.

Kingsway Infant school was much smaller than the junior school which Alfie attended. Only 79 children went to the infant school, and there were just 34 children in Megan's year, split into two classes.

However, judging by how crammed the school's car-park was by the time Alfie and his family finally arrived, it seemed as though all 79 pupils had turned up for the fete. After spending a few minutes looking for a parking space, Mr Jones gave up and decided it would be quicker to park on a road and walk. Even the surrounding roads were quite busy, though, and in the end the nearest space that Mr Jones could find was a good ten-minute walk away.

"This is your fault for taking so long to get ready," Megan complained miserably to her brother as they got out of the car and began the long walk in the bitter cold. "Father Christmas better still have some good presents or you'll be sorry."

Alfie stuck his tongue out at his little sister. This only served to make Megan even more annoyed with him. Although he got a bit of telling off from his Dad for being mean to his sister, Alfie didn't really mind – it was worth it.

Most of the fete was being held in the school's assembly hall, located just opposite the main reception area. In the hall there were stalls selling mince pies and Santa- and Rudolph-shaped cakes; there was a tombola where you could win prizes if you managed to pull out a raffle ticket ending in a zero or a five; there were a few tables selling various bits of jumble which had been donated by parents; and in one corner of the hall there was even a small bouncy castle.

Yet, despite all these attractions, the hall was strangely quiet – especially given how many cars were parked outside.

This was because most of the children were queuing to get into Megan's classroom, which for the afternoon had been transformed into Santa's Grotto.

"Ohhh. Now I'll have to wait ages until I can see Father Christmas. Thanks Alfie!" Megan moaned.

Alfie thought about responding by blowing a raspberry at his sister, but a stern look from his Dad made him think twice. He wisely decided to say and do nothing.

It took Megan about 30 minutes before she got to the front of the queue. She had spent most of that time sulking and whining about Alfie. Now that she was the next person to go into the Grotto, though, her mood had improved dramatically, and she had started bouncing around again like she had been at home.

"Are you going to go in and see Santa, darling?" Mrs Jones asked her son once Megan had disappeared excitedly into the specially decorated classroom.

"May as well now I'm here, I suppose," answered Alfie. "Got nothing better to do have I?" he added, trying to sound cool – and failing.

"Well, if you're not that bothered about going in we could always go and have a look in the hall while your Mum waits for your sister to come out," offered Mr Jones.

Alfie suddenly started to worry that he had played things too cool. "No. No, it's okay," he said, quickly changing his tone of voice from one of complete calm to one bordering on excitement. "I'll see Santa; I don't mind that much, really. Honest."

Mr and Mrs Jones shared a secret smile with each other. They knew their son well enough to know that he still liked seeing Father Christmas, even if he did pretend otherwise.

Moments later, Megan came out of the Grotto clutching a teddy bear. She looked happy enough with her present so Alfie figured that he wouldn't be in her bad books anymore. He wasn't sure whether this was a good thing or not.

"Your turn then, Alf," said Mr Jones.

Although Alfie didn't bound through the classroom door quite as fast or as excitedly as Megan had done, he didn't exactly slouch slowly through it, either.

Once inside the Grotto, the first thing that Alfie noticed was that it didn't look particularly Christmassy. This was strange seeing as how much effort had gone into making the outside of the classroom look like a real Santa's Grotto.

He then noticed something even stranger. There was no Father Christmas inside the Grotto. There weren't even any elves. He was just standing in an empty classroom.

"Hello! Santa?" Alfie called out nervously. "Santa, where are you? Is there anybody..." But before Alfie could finish his sentence, he got a strange tingling sensation in his spine.

All of a sudden, the classroom started to fill up with smoke and he began to hear a familiar sound – the tinkling of wind chimes.

Seconds later the smoke cleared, the wind chimes hushed, and standing there, right in front of Alfie, was none other than Madam Zola.

Chapter eleven

"Surprise," beamed Madam Zola, raising both of her hands high in the air. They didn't stay aloft for long, though. For within seconds of making her grand entrance, Madam Zola started to cough heavily.

"Oh no, not again! I'm really getting fed up with all this bloomin' smoke," she spluttered to herself in between coughs.

So shocked was Alfie to see the fortune teller standing right there in front of him, that it took the young boy a moment or two before he felt able to speak.

Even then he couldn't quite find the words he needed in order to ask all the

questions he wanted to. "But... What....
How...." Was all he was able to muster.

"Would you like to know what I'm doing
here, Alfie?" Madam Zola asked, smiling
a friendly smile. She then broke into yet
another fit of coughs.

Not trusting that he would be able to
get his words out to be able to answer
the fortune teller properly, Alfie simply
nodded.

The old woman cleared her throat one
final time, the coughing fit having finally
stopped. "I just wanted to see how you
are," she replied, sounding genuinely
concerned. "You looked so miserable
when I saw you in the park last Sunday. I
wanted to check that you were okay."

"So it was you that I saw?" Alfie said,
more to himself than to her. He was
slowly starting to feel more composed
as the initial shock of seeing the fortune
teller in the Grotto, instead of Father
Christmas, began to wear off.

The old woman looked confused for a
second or two, then smiled again. "Of
course it was me, silly. Who else could it
have been?"

"But why were you there? And why
did you leave so quickly?" Alfie asked,
thinking back to Madam Zola's sudden

disappearance. "I was about to walk over and say hello to you."

The fortune teller thought for a bit. "Let's just say that I had some business that I needed to attend to," she answered after a short pause.

"Hmmm," responded Alfie, obviously not quite satisfied with the vague answer that he had been given. "What kind of business?"

For the first time since Alfie had met her, the tone of Madam Zola's voice changed. "Nothing that is of concern to you," she snapped.

Instead of sounding friendly and welcoming, as she always had done before, the old woman suddenly sounded very annoyed and bad tempered. The good-natured smile also disappeared from her face momentarily, and for the briefest of moments she looked really, really angry.

Alfie thought back to the first time he had seen Madam Zola and how at first she'd reminded him a little bit of a witch. That feeling returned now.

Whatever it was Madam Zola had been doing that morning she clearly didn't want to discuss it with Alfie.

The look of anger on the fortune teller's

face didn't last much longer than a couple of seconds. Without even taking a breath the friendly tone immediately returned to her voice. "I take it you've cheered up a bit now after playing so well in the second half against Brook Wanderers. A real man-of-the-match performance, wasn't it?"

"Yeah, I was really good," Alfie enthused, already forgetting Madam Zola's sudden change of character now that he had a chance to talk about football. "I set up a goal and would have scored one as well but one of my teammates kicked the ball in the goal before..."

He stopped before finishing the sentence. Something was bothering him. "Who told you that I played well?"

"Nobody told me, Alfie. As I told you at the funfair, I know everything about you. Isn't it good news that you're starting the game tomorrow?"

Once again Alfie found himself speechless. How was it possible that she knew all this? He had only found out that he would be in the team for definite that very morning. Yet the fortune teller already knew that he would be playing.

He should have been scared of this

strange woman. But for some reason he wasn't. He was amazed by her.

The fortune teller laughed in an amused manner. "You look just like you did at the fair when I told you some of the things I knew about you. I really would have thought you'd be used to me knowing everything by now."

Alfie was still unable to speak. He just stared into the old woman's dark brown eyes. They seemed to be twinkling even more than they usually did. She seemed to be really enjoying the young boy's reaction to her powers. The anger that had been present only a few minutes ago was well and truly gone now.

"Oh, by the way, I think you're right not to trust Jasper and Keith," Madam Zola continued. "They are definitely up to something."

"Do you know what?" Alfie asked straight away. The chance to find out what Keith and Jasper were planning was enough to help him overcome his latest bout of speechlessness.

But Madam Zola didn't answer. She was distracted by something else. Her right hand was poking around for something in a pocket of her purple gown while her left hand was raised, the palm pointing towards Alfie in order to hush him.

"Did you hear me? Do you know what Jasper and Keith are up to?" Alfie tried again. His voice was sounding increasingly whiney, just like it did when he was trying to ask his Mum or Dad something when they were busy dealing with Megan and not really listening to what he was saying.

"Shhh," was Madam Zola's response.

After about half-a-minute of increasingly frantic searching, she finally found what it was she was looking for. Out of the pocket she pulled a teddy bear dressed in a blue football kit, not too dissimilar to the one the Kingsway Colts played in. "Here. Take this," she said handing the teddy bear to Alfie.

"What is it?" The young boy asked, clearly confused by the gift.

"Why it's your present from Santa, silly" answered the fortune teller as if was totally obvious why she had given him a teddy bear.

"Yeah, but..."

"Look..." Said Madam Zola cutting him off. She suddenly seemed hurried, as if she had somewhere else to be. "...It will bring you good luck, providing you don't tell anybody about seeing me today.

That's very important, Alfie, you must not tell anybody you've seen me! Nobody at all. As far as everyone else is concerned, you've been to see Santa and he gave you this teddy bear. But it really is lucky, Alfie, you just need to tell it the one thing you really want to happen."

"What do you mean?" Alfie asked. He sounded desperately confused. "What do you mean tell it the one thing I really want to happen? I don't understand."

"No time to explain. You'll have to work that out for yourself," said the fortune teller. She was now looking at her left wrist, as if checking for the time, even though she was not wearing a watch. "I've really got to go now."

Before he could reply Alfie started to hear wind chimes once again.

"Oh, I almost forgot. There is one more thing," said Madam Zola quickly as the clanging of the wind chimes started to get louder and louder.

"Yes?" Alfie cried eagerly. He was sure the fortune teller was finally going to tell him something useful.

"How is Des's ankle?"

Alfie was taken aback. "It's fine. He just sprained it really badly."

Just then, a horrible thought entered

the young boy's mind. "Wait. Please tell me you didn't have anything to do with Des hurting himself. You didn't, did you Madam Zola?" Now it was Alfie's turn to sound very cross.

But before the fortune teller had time to answer him, smoke had once again started to fill the room.

When it cleared a moment or so later, Madam Zola was gone. Alfie was standing alone in Megan's classroom, clutching a teddy bear dressed in a blue football kit.

Chapter twelve

With the warning from Madam Zola still ringing in his ears, Alfie, as instructed, kept quiet about his meeting with the fortune teller.

He did ask his Mum and Dad if they had heard wind chimes while they were standing outside Megan's classroom, but they both told him that they hadn't heard a thing.

"It was probably Rudolph's sleigh bells, darling," Mrs Jones assured him, patting his curly blond hair affectionately.

Before he went to sleep that night, Alfie spent a few minutes telling his new teddy bear about some of the things he really wanted. Although talking to the toy did make him feel more than a little foolish, he strongly believed that his present from Madam Zola would bring him good luck.

'After all,' reasoned Alfie to himself, 'she obviously has special powers. The bear must be magic, just like she is!'

There were numerous things that Alfie could think of that he wanted, so he decided to tell the bear about all of them. 'You never know', he thought, 'I might be really lucky and get more than one of the things'.

However, when he awoke the following morning nothing seemed to have changed.

There were no new football boots waiting for him, the latest England shirt that he'd told the bear he wanted hadn't appeared and Megan was still as annoying as ever.

In truth, Alfie didn't really think telling the bear that he wished his sister was less annoying would actually work. But he figured it was worth a try anyway.

There was only one other thing that he had told the bear he really wanted to happen. He wanted to score a hat-trick against Heath Hill United. This was what he wanted more than anything else.

Sitting at the breakfast table that morning, Alfie was more excited than he'd been for a very long time.

Not only was he actually going to be starting for the Colts later that day, but he was also convinced that, because of his magic teddy bear, he'd also score three goals as well.

"You're in a good mood this morning, Alf," said Mr Jones as Alfie wolfed down his Coco Pops.

"Yep. I'm definitely going to score my first goal today, Dad. I just know I am," answered Alfie cheerfully. "Who knows, I may even score a hat-trick? That would be cool, wouldn't it?"

Alfie's Dad was not entirely sure what a hat-trick was, but not wanting to admit this to Alfie he simply told his son that he would keep his fingers crossed for him.

A little later on, whilst sitting in the back of Mr Morris's car on the way to Heath Hill's ground, Alfie hardly said a word to either Billy or his friend's Dad.

He was too busy daydreaming about how he was going to score the perfect hat-trick – one goal with his right foot, one with his left foot and the other with his head.

There was no doubt in his mind that he

would not score a hat-trick in the game. Nothing else he had told the teddy bear had happened and this was all that was left.

Alfie decided that this must have been the reason why the bear was wearing what looked like a Kingsway Colts kit. It was Madam Zola's way of hinting to him what he should tell the toy.

Just to make sure that the bear would definitely bring him good luck, Alfie had placed the fortune teller's gift in the bottom of his football bag.

Although there was no way he would take it out of the bag in front of any of his teammates – he feared they would all make fun of him, especially Jasper – just having it close by made Alfie feel far more confident. And as the Colts' former coach old Jimmy Grimshaw had once told the team: "Confidence is one of the most important assets that a footballer possesses."

"What are you thinking about, Alf?" Billy asked him as Mr Morris's car entered the small village of Heath Hill, located on the outskirts of Kingsway. "You've hardly said a word all the way here."

"Oh, nothing really," Alfie answered.

He wanted to tell his best friend all about Madam Zola and how he knew he was going to score a hat-trick today. But he knew he couldn't. Madam Zola had warned him that if he told anyone about his meeting with her then the bear wouldn't bring him good luck.

There was no way he was going to allow that to happen. He was desperate to score a hat-trick.

"You must be really excited to be playing, Alfie," said Mr Morris. "It's nothing more than you deserve. Maybe Keith's finally going to start being fair to you. I hope so, because a lot of the parents were starting to get fed up with him last week."

Alfie thought back to the look on Mr Morris's face after Keith had blamed Billy for Jasper's appalling shot in the previous week's game. Billy's Dad was certainly one of the parents who was getting fed up with Keith; there could be little doubt about that.

"Even Jasper's been nice to you this week at school, hasn't he, Alf?" Billy said.

Alfie had to agree. Jasper hadn't been horrible to him once since last Sunday and had even picked him to be on his team at the previous day's training session. It was the first time this had ever happened.

But Alfie still didn't trust Jasper. Or his father. He couldn't help but remember the way Keith and Jasper had looked at him after the Brook Wanderers match or the way Keith had smiled at him after telling him he would be in the team for today's game. Even Madam Zola had warned him about them.

But while he still couldn't figure out what it was they were planning, Alfie knew it wouldn't be too long before he found out.

Chapter thirteen

Mr Morris's car, as was so often the case, was the first belonging to any of the Colts' parents to arrive at Heath Hill's ground.

Billy's Dad always liked to leave his house slightly early "just in case the traffic's bad." It never was, though, so Alfie and Billy were often the first players to arrive – especially to away matches.

Usually, upon arriving at the ground, the two boys would get out of the car and go and have a quick kick-around on the pitch while they waited for the rest of their teammates to turn up. Yet it was so cold on that particular December morning that they decided to stay in the car with Mr Morris and enjoy the car's heating a while longer.

Their reprieve from the cold didn't last long. Within seconds of Mr Morris's arrival, Chloe's Mum drove into the car park, quickly followed by Liam's Dad. Pranav's parents were the next to arrive and when the car belonging to the Mum and Dad of the Colts' best defender, Danny Foreman, pulled into the Heath Hill Village Green car park around five minutes later, all of the Colts players were present and ready to play.

All, that is, except for one noticeable exception. Jasper was nowhere to be seen. Neither was his father.

"They'll have to get here soon," Billy commented to Alfie and Liam as the three boys took turns shooting at Pranav in goal. "There are only a few minutes until kick-off and we haven't got any subs today. If Jasper doesn't get here soon we'll only have six players instead of seven."

"We won't have a coach, either," added Liam.

Alfie nodded. But he wasn't really bothered by Jasper and Keith's absence. In fact, he actually felt quite relieved about them not being there. Whatever it was that those two had planned for him they wouldn't be able to do it if they weren't there.

The trio's conversation was suddenly interrupted by the shrill sound of the referee's whistle.

"I'm not standing around here any longer. It's freezing," shouted the ref – a parent of one of the Heath Hill players. "You'll just have to start the game with one player less. If anyone else turns up then they can join in if and when they get here."

No sooner had the ref said these words, did Keith's car suddenly come screeching into the car park, sending gravel flying into the other parked cars. Much to the annoyance of the parents of children from both teams.

Almost before the car had even stopped, both its front doors were flung open, and out jumped Keith and Jasper, who began hurriedly making their way towards the pitch.

"Sorry ref," called out Keith. "We got lost. We don't know this area too well. I'm their coach; can I have a quick word with my team before you get underway?"

"Hurry up, then," the ref shouted back, clearly annoyed that he'd now have to wait a little bit longer to start the match.

"I'll give you two minutes to get sorted. No more"

Keith called the team into a huddle and gave them a very quick team-talk. He was just about to send them to line up in their usual positions when he suddenly turned to Alfie.

"Jones, what are you doing in that kit?" the manager asked him.

Alfie looked confused. "You said I'd be starting yesterday at training. And we've only got seven players so there are no subs today."

"Oh, silly me," said Keith, slapping his forehead in an overdramatic fashion. "I can't believe I forgot to tell you. Can you believe it Jasper? Oh, how stupid of me. I am silly. " The manager looked at his son and shrugged his shoulders.

"You are silly, Dad," answered Jasper, returning his father's shrug of the shoulders. The same unpleasant smile that father and son had shared a week earlier had returned to both their faces.

"What did you forget to tell me?" Alfie asked, frowning. He already knew he wasn't going to like the answer.

"When I said you'd be starting, I meant you'd be starting in goal. I can't believe I forgot to tell you." Keith laughed wickedly for a moment and then adopted a far more serious tone. "Pranav, swap shirts with him quickly. Hurry up now. The ref's waiting for you."

Both Alfie and Pranav looked at Keith with disbelief. The Colts' usual goalkeeper didn't want to play on pitch anymore than Alfie wanted to play in goal.

" Hurry up now you two," said Keith, ignoring the pleas of the two boys who didn't want to swap shirts or positions. "It's only fair that we all share positions, isn't it? I'm sure that's what your old coach used to do. I bet none of you used to moan then."

The referee's whistle sounded again. "Come on now. Let's get going. I'm turning into a block of ice over here," he called over.

Begrudgingly, Alfie and Pranav did what they were told and swapped shirts. Keith smiled again. This time the smile looked even meaner than it had looked previously.

Alfie couldn't believe it. There would be no hat-trick for him, after all.

The 'magic' bear hadn't worked.

Madam Zola had been wrong.

Chapter fourteen

While Alfie may not have been a substitute for once, he may as well have been.

The game was over halfway through the first half and he was yet to touch the ball. Heath Hill were not a very good team and the Colts were already three goals in front – Liam had scored two and Chloe one. Billy had set all three up.

The home side had so far struggled to get the ball into the Colts' half, let alone their penalty area. Alfie was therefore bored – as well as extremely miserable.

'It's not fair', Kingsway's reluctant goalkeeper thought to himself as he watched Billy dribble around two Heath Hill defenders with ease. 'They're rubbish. I bet I would have scored a hat-trick today if I was playing on pitch.'

To make matters even worse for Alfie, he was absolutely freezing. Keith had left it so late to tell him he would be going in goal that he hadn't had a chance to put some tracksuit bottoms on or even find a tee-shirt to wear underneath his goalkeeper jersey.

Pranav, meanwhile, was still wearing the heavily padded goalkeeper tracksuit bottoms that his parents had bought him during the week, which was making it difficult for him to run.

Alfie thought about asking Keith if he could swap places with Pranav for the second half, but he knew there was no chance that his coach would say yes. Alfie realised that this was what Keith and Jasper had planned for him all along. It was no secret that Alfie hated going in goal – he was always the last to volunteer to do so at training.

But for some reason, Jasper didn't like Alfie and because of that Keith had no intention of ever being fair to him.

Another five minutes passed by, during which time the Colts added a fourth goal to their tally – Billy getting his name on the score sheet, as he seemed to most weeks. Alfie still hadn't had a touch of the ball and by now he was so cold and fed-up that he was seriously thinking about quitting the Colts for good.

As he stood there watching his teammates run rings around Heath Hill's hardworking, but ultimately not very good players, Alfie thought long and hard about what Madam Zola had told him the first time they had met. If he didn't stay with the Colts then he wouldn't fulfil his destiny of one day becoming a professional footballer.

He had managed to get into the team now, even if it was only as a goalkeeper, so Alfie figured that his Dad would no longer be in a position to force him to join Ashgate Athletic after Christmas. The deal had been that he had to get into the Colts' team by Christmas – and he had managed to do this. A deal's a deal. Mr Jones had said so himself.

But Alfie was now unsure about whether or not he really wanted to stay at the Colts when he spent so much time feeling unhappy. He knew he was good enough to play on pitch regularly and he didn't even care what position he played in – just so long as he wasn't in goal. If he joined Ashgate he would almost certainly get to play on pitch most weeks and would no doubt enjoy playing for that team a whole lot more than he did his present one.

At the same time, though, he could not quite shake Madam Zola's warning from his mind. What if he did leave the Colts? Would that mean that his chance of ever being a professional footballer would be gone for good?

Playing football for a living was something Alfie had long dreamed of doing – way before he ever met the fortune teller. Was it worth risking his dream just because he was feeling a little dejected?

Then again, thought Alfie, the fortune teller had told him that the bear she had given him would bring him good luck if he told it what he really wanted. He had tried this, yet nothing had happened. Maybe the mysterious old woman didn't have any special powers after all. Maybe leaving the Colts wouldn't affect his supposed destiny any more than staying with them would.

Who knew if it was really his destiny to be a professional footballer anyway? It wasn't out of the question that Madam Zola could have been wrong.

Alfie didn't know what to think or do for the best.

All these thoughts were passing through his mind when he suddenly realised that something unusual had happened. Heath Hill had managed to get the ball into the Colts' half and they were actually on the attack.

What's more, because Kingsway had been so on top during the match, Danny hadn't bothered to stay in defence like he was supposed to, meaning the Heath Hill striker was clean through on goal with only Alfie to beat.

He may not have liked playing in goal, but Alfie watched enough football matches on TV to know what he should do next. Without even thinking he started to run towards the striker, hoping to hurry the attacker into taking a shot while at the same time narrowing the angle so that the opposition player had a smaller target to aim at.

It worked. The Heath Hill number seven was not used to being through on goal and Alfie's sudden presence in front of him panicked the striker into taking a shot before he was ready to do so.

With so little of the goal to aim for the strike would need to be precise if it was to beat Alfie.

Fortunately it wasn't.

In fact, the ball ended up closer to the corner flag than it did to the intended target. As the number seven trudged off towards the halfway line, his head in his hands as his teammates tried to encourage him despite such a woeful attempt, Alfie rushed off to get the ball from behind the goal.

Finally he was going to get a kick of the match ball.

Or so he thought.

Despite the fact he'd ran about 20 yards to get the ball, when he got back to his penalty area Jasper was already waiting there to take the goal kick.

"Come on muppet give me the ball," the Colts' captain demanded, ripping the ball out of Alfie's hands before the goalkeeper even had a chance to give it to him. "You know I take goal kicks. I've got the hardest kick!"

Alfie despondently walked back to his goal. It was nearly half-time and he still hadn't touched the ball – at least not properly. He looked up as Jasper began his run up to launch the ball up field.

Only that's not quite what happened.

As was so often the case when Jasper took a goal kick, the ball didn't go anywhere near where he wanted it to. In fact, on this occasion, the ball didn't even go forward. Instead, Jasper hopelessly sliced the ball back towards his own goal. Before Alfie even knew what had happened it had flown past him and into the net.

Jasper almost exploded with rage. His whole face went a bright shade of red, just like Keith's did when he was angry, and his whole body began to shake. "You did that on purpose," yelled Jasper, sounding as if he was just about to cry. "I tried to pass the ball to you and you just let it go into the goal." Alfie wasn't certain, but he thought he could see tears in his captain's eyes.

"Come off it, Jasper," said Billy running over to stick up for his best friend. "There was nothing he could have done about that. It was your fault."

Alfie was just about to agree when he heard Keith shout from the sideline. "Jones what are you doing? Can't you even control a simple pass? I don't know why you bother turning up, I really don't."

97

It was at that exact moment that Alfie made his mind up for good. This would definitely be his last game for the Colts.

Chapter fifteen

While it was far from unusual for Keith
to blame others for his son's mistakes,
this time he had gone too far.

All of the Colts players – aside from
Jasper – had rushed over to console
Alfie, who had sunk to his knees and was
refusing to get up.

Jasper stood alone on the edge of the
centre circle with his arms folded. He
was still furious about the own goal he
had just scored. Even though he was
convinced he was totally blameless for his
part in it.

Alfie's gloved hands were pressed
tightly over his face. He was desperately

trying to stem the flow of tears that had begun to spring from his eyes almost immediately after Keith had shouted at him.

The ref blew his whistle in an attempt to get the team's attention so that they could restart the game. If any of the Colts' players had heard the whistle, they didn't show it. None of them moved more than a centimetre away from their distraught goalkeeper, while Jasper remained rooted to the spot where he was standing.

Having failed to get their attention by blowing his whistle, the ref walked over to where the players were gathered around Alfie. Seeing that the goalkeeper was so upset he decided that rather than restarting the game for the two minutes of the half that remained, he would blow his whistle for half-time slightly early instead.

No one involved with the Colts even noticed.

While Billy, Liam, Pranav, Chloe and Danny all tried their best to comfort Alfie on the pitch, on the sideline all of the Colts' players' parents had marched angrily over to where Keith was standing.

"That's totally unfair," Mr Morris told

Keith, as behind him the other parents echoed and nodded their agreement. "That was Jasper's fault. Not Alfie's. Just like it was Jasper's bad shot that caused him to miss a chance last week, not Billy's poor pass."

For a second, Keith looked stunned by what Mr Morris had said. He quickly regained his composure. "I don't know what you're talking about," he spat back at the group of parents who had gathered to face him.

"I'm talking about how every week you blame others for your son's mistakes," continued Mr Morris, trying hard not to raise his voice. "Not that it matters when he makes a mistake. Everybody does. No one is perfect. It's just not fair to blame others. That's all I'm saying."

Once again the other parents all backed up what Mr Morris had just said.

Keith didn't answer straight away. He looked at the parents with a look of utter disbelief on his face.

"Are you telling me I don't know what I'm talking about?" the manager finally replied. He looked and sounded really cross now. The colour of his face had turned from its usual shade of red to more of a beetroot purple. "Since I've taken over this team, we haven't lost one single game. That also means that since Jasper joined the Colts, the team hasn't lost. Yet you don't like the way I'm running things? What, would you rather, the team lost every week... like it used to under the old coach?"

Mr Morris thought long and hard about his answer before replying. He really didn't want to get angry with Keith. Not in front of the children. What sort of an example would that be to set to them?

Thankfully none of the Colts players had even noticed that there was an argument going on – most were still too busy trying to cheer Alfie up, while Jasper was still standing alone on the edge of the centre circle stomping his feet. Much like a toddler throwing a paddy.

"Look, Keith," Mr Morris began, trying his hardest to stay calm. "It's not all about winning for the kids. Not at their age. What's just as important is that the children enjoy themselves... and at the moment I'm not really sure that they are." For the third time, all the other parents agreed with him.

Keith let what he was hearing sink in for a minute. "Are you saying that they prefer losing to winning?" he asked, sounding genuinely baffled.

"That's not exactly what I'm saying. What I mean is, they need to enjoy playing so that they..." Billy's Dad started to explain what he meant, but before he could finish he was interrupted by the referee.

"I'm not sure what's going on here," the ref began cautiously, "but is your team going to be in a position to play the second half or not?" Unsurprisingly, the ref seemed more than a little nervous about having to approach the group of warring parents, but as he explained, "it's freezing cold and if you don't want to continue then I'd like to know so we can all go home and get warm."

"Sorry ref," said Keith, trying, but failing, to adopt a friendly tone. He didn't once take his eyes off Mr Morris or the other parents. "I think we're done here. It was just a little misunderstanding. Wasn't it?"

Mr Morris reluctantly nodded, and eventually so did the other parents. They all knew that an angry confrontation would not do anybody any good in the long run.

The ref looked at them doubtfully but told the parents that they had two minutes to sort out whatever problems it was that they were having. If the Colts weren't ready to play by the time he blew his whistle to start the second half, then he would just abandon the match.

Keith turned away from the parents for the first time since they had approached him and looked towards the pitch. "Okay you lot, in you come. Quickly. We haven't got much time," he yelled to his team.

While Jasper sprinted over to his Dad the moment he heard his voice, none of the other children moved. They had spent five minutes trying to cheer Alfie up, but nothing they said had worked.

They were now talking about whether they should bother carrying on with the game. Billy and Pranav thought they shouldn't, Danny and Liam thought they should, Chloe wasn't sure. In the end they decided it should be up to Alfie to decide whether or not they should play the second half.

"It's up to you, Alf," said Billy. "We'll not bother playing the rest of the game if you don't want us to."

It was then that Alfie removed his hands from his eyes for the first time.

Both of his blue eyes were completely bloodshot from where he'd been crying so much, but the tears had stopped now and Alfie, despite the puffiness around his eyes, looked strangely relaxed.

"Let's finish the game," he said, without so much as a tremor in his voice. Not only did he look relaxed, he sounded totally calm as well.

"Are you sure, Alf?" Billy continued. "I mean, we really don't have to if you don't want to."

"I'm sure," he replied, just as Keith called for them a second time. "Go over to him. I want to be alone for a minute."

Billy told his friend that he'd stay with him, but Alfie again insisted that he wanted to be alone.

Once the other five players had joined Keith on the sideline, Alfie raced over to the other side of the pitch where his bag was buried underneath a pile of other bags.

Once he had located which of the seemingly identical blue sport bags actually belonged to him, he began rummaging around in it until he finally pulled out the item he was looking for.

Alfie looked at his supposedly lucky bear and smiled.

He finally knew what he really wanted to happen.

Chapter sixteen

Perhaps unsurprisingly, the second half was a far more even affair than the first half had been.

For the second week running, most of the Colts players looked like they weren't enjoying playing football, and once again the reason for their unhappiness stemmed from Keith's rough treatment of Alfie.

Even Jasper didn't seem his normal committed self. Although the reason for his lack of attention towards the game was very different to that of his teammates. The Colts' captain couldn't stop thinking about his own goal. The more he thought about it, the angrier he became. And the angrier he became, the more he blamed Alfie for letting the ball go past him and into the net.

In Jasper's opinion, Alfie had let the ball go into the goal on purpose, just to make him look foolish. Every time he replayed the incident in his head, the more convinced he became of how easy it would have been for Alfie to stop the ball from hitting the back of the net.

The reality, however, was that even the best goalkeeper in the world would have struggled to save the ball, so woefully sliced and powerfully struck had the goal kick been.

Jasper would never see it that way, though. So, rather than concentrating on the game going on around him, he was instead thinking of ways he could get Alfie back for letting the ball in.

Strangely, the only player on the Colts team who looked to be even remotely enjoying the second half, was Alfie. With his team not really interested in the game anymore, Heath Hill had actually managed to have a couple of shots on target, both of which Alfie had saved.

The second save was a particularly good one, with Alfie getting his fingertips to a well struck shot which had looked to have been heading for the bottom corner of the net. Due to his lack of height, Alfie had had to really stretch to be able to get his hands on the ball, and this made the save look even more impressive. Parents from both teams applauded the save and even Keith nodded his approval, much to Jasper's obvious disgust.

In all, though, Alfie still didn't have that much to do in the second half. Even a subdued Colts team were far too good for Heath Hill, and with only seconds of the match remaining, Liam completed his hat-trick with a powerful shot from the edge of the penalty area.

The referee blew the full-time whistle soon after. But while the final score may have been 5-1 to the Colts, no one really felt like celebrating the victory. Most of the players were still feeling down about the events which had occurred during the match, while the watching parents were also quieter than usual following their confrontation with Keith.

It was only Alfie who seemed to be pleased by the result. Having shaken hands with all of the opposition players, the Colts' goalkeeper ran over to Billy who was walking towards his Dad. "Hey

Bill, great result, wasn't it?" he said cheerfully, completely taking his friend by surprise.

"Er, yeah, it was alright I suppose. You okay now?"

"Yeah, I'm good," Alfie smiled back.

Billy looked puzzled. "But what about what Keith said to you? I thought he'd really upset you. I mean you were crying and everything."

Alfie was just about to deny that he had been crying – he was a little bit embarrassed that so many of his friends had seen him in tears – but quickly figured there was no point in doing so; they had seen him cry and that was that. "Yeah, well, I don't think we're going to have to worry about Keith for much longer."

"Really? Why do you think that?"

Alfie shrugged his shoulders. "Just do."

Right then, seemingly from out of nowhere, Jasper appeared in front of them.

"You think you're so clever, don't you, muppet?" said the larger boy angrily. The colour of Jasper's face had gone back to the same angry shade of red that it had been just after he'd scored the own goal.

"I do actually," Alfie replied cheekily. He

was smiling broadly, desperately trying to make it look like he was not scared of Jasper. Inside, though, he could feel his heart thumping hard against his chest, while he could also feel his legs starting to shake.

"You're going to pay for letting me score an own goal. I'll get you back for that. Nobody makes Jasper Johnson look foolish."

Alfie said the first thing that came into his head. He just couldn't stop himself. "No. You can do a good enough job of that on your own, can't you Jasper?"

Alfie wasn't sure where this new-found bravery was coming from, while even Jasper was momentarily lost for words by Alfie's sudden boldness. Billy chuckled loudly. Something which only made Jasper angrier than he already was.

The larger boy pushed Alfie hard in the chest, causing the smaller boy to double up in pain.

"Oi, stop that," shouted Mr Morris, who had been keeping an eye on the three boys from the moment Jasper had stood in front of Billy and Alfie.

The shout had been loud enough to catch the attention of most of the other parents and children who were still standing in the car park, all of whom now turned to see what was going on.

"Whatever," Jasper sneered. The bully began to walk towards his Dad who had been talking to the referee and was now walking in the direction of the commotion.

"What's going on?" Keith asked as he approached his son.

"Alfie pushed me so I pushed him back," Jasper lied.

"That's not what happened at all," said Mr Morris. "I saw the whole thing. Jasper pushed him for no reason."

"Are you calling my son a liar?" Keith seemed furious that Billy's Dad would suggest that his angel of a son would do something so nasty without being provoked.

"Well, yes, I am actually, because I saw exactly what happened."

"So did I," ventured Billy. Alfie said nothing – he was still in too much pain and was struggling to get his breath back following Jasper's shove. The larger boy's hand had caught him right in the stomach and had left him badly winded.

By now, quite a crowd had gathered to see what was going on. Within seconds the parents of the Colts players were arguing with Keith, their children were arguing with Jasper – things were threatening to get out of hand.

And then one person's voice hushed everything.

"Just what exactly is going on here?" yelled a deep, booming voice.

The arguing adults and children stopped squabbling with each other immediately and turned to look at who had spoken – although almost everybody already knew exactly who it was.

And sure enough, standing right behind them, was a very unimpressed looking Jimmy Grimshaw.

Chapter seventeen

Jimmy Grimshaw did not look at all
amused.

The old man was standing bolt upright
with his arms folded tight. He was
shaking his head furiously from side to
side and his already heavily wrinkled
face was even more creased than usual.
He looked very different to how he did
the last time the Colts' players and their
parents had seen him.

It had been over two months since
Jimmy had been taken ill and forced to
quit his position as coach of the Kingsway
Colts under 9s. All those who now found
themselves looking at him were unsure

as to whether his change in appearance was down to his illness or his bad mood. Nobody, not the parents or their children, could ever remember having seen the old man angry before, so patient and kindly had he always been towards all of them.

"Well?" Jimmy snapped, when after a few seconds it became clear that nobody was in a hurry to answer him. "Is somebody going to tell me what's going on here or not?"

Still no answer was forthcoming. Everyone looked down at the floor and said nothing. Not only were they all desperate to avoid Jimmy's harsh stare, but they – the parents especially – were also embarrassed about being caught arguing so loudly in public.

Jimmy was just about to demand for the third time an answer to what exactly was going on, when he suddenly noticed that Alfie was still curled up in a ball on the floor.

So distracted had everyone been at arguing with one another that no one had actually thought to check on how Alfie was feeling following Jasper's shove.

Old Jimmy rushed over to Alfie straight away and put a friendly hand on his back. "Take it easy Alfie," said the former coach warmly. "Just take some deep breaths in and out and you'll soon be fine."

Alfie did as he was told and sure enough in no time whatsoever he started to feel a little better. "Thanks Jimmy," said Alfie once he'd got his breath back enough to be able to talk. "It's good to see you. I knew you'd come. I knew you wouldn't let me down."

Jimmy didn't really understand what Alfie meant by this. He hadn't spoken to anyone about coming or going anywhere, but he decided there was no rush to ask the boy what he was talking about.

He had more important things he

wanted to find out first.

"So, Alfie, do you want to tell me what's going on here as no one else seems to able to speak right now?" He said this just loud enough for all the onlookers to hear. Once again everyone looked a little embarrassed. Even the parents looked like naughty school children who had just been told off by their teacher.

But before Alfie had a chance to answer his former coach, someone from the group of the up-to-now silent adults finally said something.

"What exactly has it got to do with you what's going on here?" It was Keith. "You haven't got anything to do with the Colts anymore."

"Yeah, you haven't got anything to do with the Colts anymore," repeated Jasper, sounding not too dissimilar to a particularly annoying parrot.

"You can't speak to him like that," replied Mr Morris angrily. "Jimmy Grimshaw has been coaching football teams longer than you've been alive, Keith. Show the man some respect."

All the other parents, and most of the children, echoed their agreement and before long another argument was in full swing.

Once again it was Jimmy who halted the quarrelling Colts. "Silence," he demanded loudly. And just like that the squabbling group quietened immediately.

"Keith has a point. I'm not the team's coach anymore," admitted the old man. "But after what I've just spent the last few minutes witnessing with my own two eyes, I really think I should be. What sort of an example is this behaviour to set to young children? It simply won't do at all. You should all be ashamed of yourselves."

Again the parents, even Keith, looked a little sheepish.

"My doctor says that I'm as fit as a fiddle and that a little bit of football coaching should do me no harm whatsoever," Jimmy continued. "So if it's okay with all of you, I'd like to be your coach again."

Most of the parents and children all cheered – no one louder than Alfie, who was evidently delighted by what Jimmy had said.

Keith looked shocked. "I'm sorry old man, but I'm the coach of the Kingsway Colts under 9s now, and I'm not giving the position up for anyone," he said. Jasper nodded his head firmly in agreement with his father. "If you want to coach this team, then you're going to have to start up a new team next season."

"Fine," said Mr Morris, before Jimmy could answer. "Then that's what you'll do, isn't it Jimmy? All the children will leave the Colts and come and play for a new team coached by you next season."

Once again almost everybody cheered. But to their surprise, rather than look happy about what Mr Morris had proposed, Jimmy Grimshaw looked incredibly sad.

Surprisingly, Alfie did not look too happy either. Not that anybody had noticed. Everyone was too busy looking at Jimmy. Alfie was thinking about what Madam Zola had said and was worried that if he didn't play for the Colts his destiny had no chance of coming true. He wasn't prepared to give up totally on what the fortune teller had told him just yet.

"No. No. No," said the old man, glumly shaking his head. "That's not what I want at all. I've been involved with the Kingsway Colts for many, many years. More than I care to remember if I'm being honest. I don't want to coach any other team. And I won't."

"Well that's just tough," said Keith.

"Because I'm not quitting as coach. Not for you. Not for anyone."

"But Keith," reasoned Mr Morris. "None of our kids will ever play for the Colts again all the time you're the coach." The other parents and their children all nodded in agreement.

"Then I guess I'll have to find some new players, won't I?" Keith replied, sounding very much like a spoilt eight- or nine-year-old himself.

"I know plenty of people who could play, Dad," said Jasper. "And they're better than any of this lot!"

Believing this to be the end of the conversation, Keith and Jasper turned towards their car, which was still not parked properly following their rushed entrance to the ground just over an hour ago. However, before they had quite reached their vehicle, Jimmy called out to them. "Wait just a minute you two."

Keith turned slowly back towards the group he had just walked away from. "What is it now old man? I think I've made my feelings perfectly clear"

"I've got an idea. Now, you strike me as the sort of man who likes a challenge."

Keith nodded but said nothing.

"Well, as luck would have it, I've got a

little challenge in mind. If you win then you can stay as coach of the Colts and all of these children will leave to join new teams or maybe even choose to start a totally new one. However, if I win, then I become coach of the Colts again and you and Jasper have to leave."

Keith slowly stroked his chin while he thought about what Jimmy was offering. "Hmmm. Okay, I may be interested. But I'm not agreeing anything until I know just what the challenge is. So what is it?"

"I don't want to tell you that just yet," said Jimmy smiling. "Turn up at training next Saturday at the usual time and I'll tell you what it is then. I'll then let you decide whether you want to go through with it or not, but I've got a really good feeling that you'll accept."

Keith thought about it some more for about thirty seconds. "Okay, old man. You're on. I'll see you all next Saturday. Come on Jasper, get in the car."

Keith and Jasper finally got in their car and drove off leaving the rest of the parents and Colts players with Jimmy. They all pleaded with their former coach to give them at least some clue of what the challenge would entail. But Jimmy was giving nothing away.

"I'm afraid you're all going to have to wait until next week," he said. And with that he waved his goodbyes and headed back the way he had come without so much as another word.

Chapter eighteen

The last week of school before the Christmas break is always more fun and exciting than any usual school week (aside from, perhaps, the week before the summer holidays).

But even without the promise of just over two weeks away from school to come, and the thrill of Christmas Day itself just around the corner, Alfie and his friends would have found this week to be particularly exciting no matter what time of year it was.

Jimmy's sudden reappearance at the previous Sunday's match, and the secret challenge he had made to Keith, had sent the children's imaginations racing. Just what did Jimmy Grimshaw have in mind?

"I think they're going to have an arm wrestle," suggested Danny.

"Well I reckon they're going to have a running race," proposed Chloe.

"No chance. They're definitely going to have a penalty shoot-out," decided Billy.

Alfie didn't have a clue what kind of challenge Jimmy would set Keith. He just hoped with all his heart that it would be one that the older man would win. He was desperate for Jimmy to become the coach of the Colts again.

It was what he wanted to happen more than anything in the world.

That this was the case had occurred to Alfie during half-time of the Heath Hill United game. Whilst lying on the ground, fighting back the tears as his teammates and friends tried their hardest to console him, Alfie had heard Chloe say that Jimmy Grimshaw would never have shouted at any of them in the way that Keith did, and how she wished he was still the team's coach.

Although he said nothing, Alfie agreed wholeheartedly with what Chloe had said. It was at that moment that it finally dawned on him what he wanted more than anything else – for Jimmy Grimshaw to be the team's coach. So once he'd finally managed to persuade his friends to go and see Keith for their half-time team talk, Alfie had rushed over to his bag to tell the bear Madam Zola had given him that he wanted Jimmy Grimshaw to return as the coach of the Kingsway Colts under 9s.

And, lo and behold, little more than half-an-hour later, Jimmy had appeared from seemingly nowhere, feeling fit and healthy and wanting to take charge of the Colts once more.

Not only had this turn of events helped to cheer Alfie up no end, it had also reassured him that Madam Zola did indeed possess magical powers. Once again, he was fully convinced that it was indeed his destiny to be a professional footballer.

However, as that final week of school dragged on and on, Alfie found himself starting to feel increasingly nervous about Jimmy's chances in a challenge against Keith.

Jimmy had seemed certain that Keith would accept the challenge, so whatever task the old man had in mind would have to appeal to the current coach. And the truth was that, if any of his friends' guesses of what the challenge would be turned out to be correct, then Jimmy would surely stand little chance of winning. Keith was much bigger, stronger and younger than the former coach. What's more, Alfie couldn't help but think that Keith would also cheat to win. Something he could never imagine Jimmy doing. Not ever.

Nevertheless, Alfie was still curious about what Jimmy had in mind, and by the last day of term it was virtually impossible to tell what the Colts players were more excited about – the Christmas holidays or Jimmy's challenge.

Even Des, who was still too injured to play football, said he was trying to convince his Mum and Dad to take him to training that Saturday, just so he could watch the challenge.

The only Colts player who didn't seem to be particularly looking forward to the challenge was Jasper. He had not spoken to any of his teammates all week. Not that he'd been bullying them, either; he had just totally ignored them. It was as if they didn't exist.

However, Jasper was obviously

confident that if his Dad did accept the old man's challenge then he would win it no matter what Jimmy had in mind. Billy had overheard the current Colts captain asking numerous children if they wanted to join his Dad's football team as they would be looking for new players after Saturday.

***

The parents of the Colts players didn't usually hang around to watch their children train on a Saturday morning.

Normally they would drop their kids off at the Kingsway Recreation Ground at 10:30, and then disappear into the nearby town centre until just before 12, when the session was due to finish.

However, the Saturday of Jimmy's challenge was a different matter altogether. By 10:20, not only were most of the children milling around the Colts' home football pitch, waiting expectantly and excitedly to find out what Jimmy had planned, but so were most of their parents as well. Despite the fact it was very cold and raining heavily.

The only parents not present were Alfie's, as they'd had to take Megan to one of her friend's Birthday parties. Even Des was there with his Mum and Dad.

By 10:30 the only people who hadn't arrived at the ground were Keith, Jasper and Jimmy Grimshaw.

"Maybe they've forgotten," said Billy to Alfie, with a shrug of his shoulders.

"Or maybe Keith's too scared to show up," replied Alfie hopefully, although he didn't really think that this would be the case.

Sure enough, the next car to arrive in the car park was Keith's. He was obviously prepared for whatever Jimmy had planned.

He and Jasper were dressed in matching tracksuits and the second Keith got out of the car he began going through an array of elaborate stretches as Jasper, who was holding a bottle of water and had a towel draped over his shoulder, clapped and shouted encouragement to his father.

After a minute of performing various stretching exercises, Keith started to jog over to where the other Colts players and their parents were standing. Jasper followed close behind, still animatedly telling his Dad that he was the best, and that there was no way he could

127

possibly lose any challenge to "old man Grimshaw."

Once the duo were about ten yards away from the rest of the group, Keith dropped to the floor and started doing some press ups. Jasper counted them and urged his father to keep going.

After doing 20 press ups Keith stood up and began jogging on the spot. Everyone else – aside from the loyal Jasper, of course – just looked on, not quite sure of what to think about the spectacle Keith was making of himself.

"So where's the old man, then?" Keith asked as he continued jogging, trying desperately to make it sound as though he wasn't in the slightest bit out of breath from all the exercise he was doing, even though he clearly was. "He's bottled it, no doubt. You lot may as well clear off home now and start looking for new teams to play for. The Colts belong to me."

"Not so fast," said a familiar voice from behind his shoulder.

Keith stopped jogging and turned to face Jimmy. To his surprise, Jimmy was not dressed for a sporting contest. He was wearing a flat cap, black shoes, smart trousers, and a big raincoat that he couldn't quite do up due to the thickness of the knitted grey woolly jumper he had on.

"You're not exactly dressed for a challenge, old boy," continued an increasingly confident looking Keith, who by now had a smirk on his face.

"On the contrary," replied Jimmy, now sounding much more like his usual calm self, far removed from the unfamiliar angry man he had appeared to be almost a week earlier. "I never said that I'd be taking part in the challenge. Just that I had a challenge in mind."

Keith, not sure what Jimmy was going on about, began to lose his temper. "I've had enough of your games now! Why don't you just tell me what it is you've got in mind. Then I can tell you whether I accept it or not."

Jimmy smiled, pleased that he had so easily managed to annoy his adversary. "My, my. That's quite a temper you've got there, Keith. You need to learn to calm down or you'll end up getting ill just like..."

"Just get on with it," bellowed Keith at the top of his voice. All the spectators, even Jasper, took a step back, shocked by the loudness and anger of Keith's outburst. Jimmy just smiled again.

"Alright. What I propose is a game of one on one football between Jasper and a boy of my choosing. We'll set up a small pitch with two little goals at either end. The first boy to score ten goals wins. Once one of them has scored five, we'll have a quick break for half-time and then swap ends."

Jimmy knew that, in Keith's eyes, Jasper could do no wrong on the football pitch. So biased was the current Colts' coach towards his son's footballing ability, that Jimmy was sure Keith would be unlikely to turn down such a challenge. He was right.

Keith's reply came without hesitation. "You're on." He looked at Jasper and smiled. Jasper smiled back at his Dad. The truth, though, was that he wasn't feeling quite as confident as he looked.

While Jasper was pretty sure he was better than most of his current teammates, even he knew he wasn't better than Billy. Not that he would ever admit it out loud.

Jasper had no doubt that Jimmy would select Billy. Nor did any of the other Colts players. They had all rushed over to Billy the second Keith had accepted Jimmy's challenge to wish him luck. Billy tried to not look too big headed, telling his teammates that Jimmy might not pick him, and that they were all as good as each other. Secretly, though, Billy was pretty sure it would be him who Jimmy would call upon to take on Jasper.

So you can imagine everyone's surprise when Jimmy didn't choose to nominate the Colts' star player.

"Come on then, Alfie," The old man called out. "Hurry up and get ready. You've got a football match to win."

Chapter nineteen

Everyone was shocked at Jimmy's decision to select Alfie for the challenge. Not least the boy himself.

Alfie had been in the process of wishing Billy luck against Jasper at the very moment Jimmy had called out his name.

At first, Alfie was sure he had simply misheard the old man. He just stood rooted to the spot, unable to move, staring disbelievingly at Jimmy. He was certain that in a moment or two his former coach would realise that he'd made a mistake and call for Billy instead.

But Alfie hadn't misheard his former coach. "Come on then, Alfie. Chop chop," urged Jimmy, clapping his hands together three times.

"Go on, then, Alf," said Billy, trying, but not quite managing, to sound as if he wasn't at all put out by not being selected for the challenge. "I'm sure you'll be fine."

Billy may not have been happy about not being chosen for the challenge, but he really did believe that his best friend would be fine. He was fully confident that Alfie could and would beat Jasper.

Alfie nodded nervously at his friend and started moving towards Jimmy. Unlike Billy, Alfie was not so sure that he'd be fine. He had butterflies in his stomach – the future of the Colts lay on his tiny shoulders and he felt sick at the thought of letting his friends and Jimmy down. Not to mention ruining his own destiny of one day becoming a professional footballer.

Jasper, on the other hand, could not quite believe his luck. He'd been preparing to face Billy; possibly Liam as he was the team's top scorer. But Alfie... well, he hadn't expected Jimmy to select him at all. Not in a million years.

Keith, too, was surprised by Jimmy's choice. He gleefully rubbed his hands together and began giving his son some final instructions. Alfie didn't like the look on Jasper's face as he listened to what his father had to say. The evil smile that Alfie has seen on his rival's face so many times before was spreading ever wider with every word Keith spoke.

Jimmy asked all the other Colts players to set up a small pitch using the training cones, and asked Mr Morris if he would mind making a goal at each end of the pitch. "Quite small goals," Jimmy advised. "About your shoulder-width apart. We want the boys to use skill and technique to score. Not power and luck."

As the others busied themselves with setting up the pitch, Jimmy crouched down so that he was at roughly the same height as Alfie. This took Jimmy some considerable time and effort as he was very tall and nowhere near as flexible as he once was.

"How are you feeling, Alfie?" Jimmy enquired.

"Fine," Alfie lied.

"Confident?" Jimmy continued.

"Yep," replied Alfie. Any more of this and he was sure it was only a matter of time before his nose started growing longer and longer.

"Look, Mr Morris has told me what a

hard time Jasper and Keith have been giving you over the past few weeks. This is your chance to show them just how unfair they've been, and prove to them just what a good player you are. Play like you can and you'll beat Jasper easily. I believe in you. We all do."

Alfie smiled broadly. Jimmy's words hadn't done anything to take away the butterflies in his stomach, but they had certainly made him feel good about himself. "Thanks Jimmy," said Alfie. "I'll do my best."

"That's all you can do, Alfie," said Jimmy, ruffling the boy's curly blonde locks with his left hand. "Give it your best effort and we'll all be proud of you, no matter what happens. Oh, and most importantly of all, go out there and enjoy it."

With this, Jimmy walked off to speak to Keith to clarify the rules of the contest.

It was agreed that each coach would ref one half of the match each; Keith the first half and Jimmy the second. The game would start with the ball being thrown into the centre of the pitch. Jasper and Alfie were to be standing on their own goal line and only allowed to move once the ball had been thrown. If the ball went off the pitch for a throw-in or goal kick, then play would restart at the feet of the boy whose throw or kick it was. Once a goal was scored the players would head back to their goal line and play would restart with the ball once again being thrown into the middle.

The rules were then explained to Jasper and Alfie. Once it was clear that both boys understood them, Keith ordered the two players to get to their goal lines so that the game could begin.

The watching crowd all gave a huge cheer as Alfie and Jasper made their ways to their starting lines. All of the

Colts players started to chant Alfie's name, and while none of the parents joined in with this chant, it was the smaller boy they were all hoping would prevail.

However, no sooner had the game started were Alfie's earlier suspicions that Keith and Jasper would try to cheat immediately proved correct.

Far from throwing the ball fairly into the middle of the pitch, as he was supposed to, Keith instead threw the ball right into Alfie's half of the pitch. Meanwhile Jasper, who was meant to have started the game on his goal line, was standing closer to the halfway line. The coach's son easily got to the ball first, and while Alfie was busy complaining to Keith that neither the initial throw nor Jasper's starting position had been fair, Jasper simply took the ball to within inches of the goal and then kicked it with all his might through the posts.

"Goal. 1-0 Jasper," said Keith.

"That's not fair," moaned Alfie. "You threw the ball into my half and Jasper wasn't even on his goal line."

"I can't help the wind can I?" said Keith, even though the wind was blowing in the opposite direction to which he'd thrown the ball. "And I didn't see Jasper's starting position as I wasn't looking."

Alfie trudged off back to his goal line, muttering angrily to himself under his breath. All of the gathered spectators started to boo. All, that is, apart from Jimmy, who shook his head sadly and then urged Alfie to keep his head up and to not give in.

Surprisingly, the next throw was fair. Alfie used his speed to get to the ball first and then cheekily put it through Jasper's legs, before nipping past him, and side footing the ball into the goal before Jasper even had a chance to turn around.

The larger boy looked at his Dad, his eyes pleading with Keith to find something wrong with the goal. But even Keith couldn't cheat that much. "Goal. 1-1," said Keith, with rather less enthusiasm than he had used when Jasper had scored only moments earlier.

The crowd cheered, and the Colts players started up their Alfie chant again. Alfie waved at the crowd, causing his friends to cheer even louder.

The next goal was almost exactly the same as the previous one. Keith again threw the ball fairly into the centre of the pitch, and even though Jasper had moved off his goal line far earlier than he was supposed to, Alfie still got to the ball first and went round Jasper with ease before scoring.

"2-1 to Alfie," said Keith barely loud enough for anyone to hear. Jasper couldn't believe it. He was losing to Alfie. He started to go red. There was no way he was going to let the smaller boy past him so easily again.

Yet it was Alfie who scored the next goal, too. This time Jasper had managed to get to the ball first – helped in no small part by the fact Keith had pretty much thrown the ball straight to his feet – but instead of trying to use some skill to get near Alfie's goal, the Colts' captain instead decided to shoot from way inside his own half.

However, the rain had made the pitch so muddy that even Jasper's hardest kick couldn't get the ball that close to the goal, and Alfie had been easily able to retrieve the ball and again use his skill to take it past Jasper and score. 3-1 to Alfie. Jasper simply couldn't believe what was happening.

"Way to go, Alfie," shouted Jimmy, clapping his hands excitedly. "Keep it up."

While everyone was busy clapping and

cheering Alfie as he made his way back to his goal line, Keith looked at Jasper and nodded. Jasper smiled back at his Dad and gave him the thumbs up.

Alfie caught a glimpse of this gesture just as he'd reached his goal line and fully expected Keith to try and cheat again with the throw. To his amazement, however, the throw was once again fair and Alfie once more reached the ball first.

He quickly decided that he was going to try and put the ball through his opponent's legs, and once again he managed to pull the trick off with ease. But this time he didn't reach the ball first. Jasper had guessed that Alfie would try this trick and had this time let the smaller boy get the ball through his legs. So when Alfie tried to run around Jasper to collect the ball he simply took a step to his right and intentionally blocked his opponent's run. Alfie was moving too fast to stop and ran straight into Jasper before falling face first into the mud.

It was a clear foul, but to no one's great surprise, Keith didn't see it that way. "Play on," shouted Keith as Jasper took control of the ball and walked it into Alfie's goal. "3-2," the coach shouted, not even trying to contain his glee.

Alfie was still on his knees when Keith threw the next ball into the middle. With no opponent to face him, Jasper again took the ball right up to the goal before smashing it as hard as he could with his right foot to make the score 3-3.

The crowd, including Jimmy, couldn't believe how unfair Keith was being. They hadn't thought that even he could cheat this much.

Alfie, covered from head to toe in mud, had finally made his way back to the goal line when Keith next restarted the game. However, he was still trying to get his breath back and was still in no fit state to compete. Although he tried his hardest to reach the ball before Jasper, it was the Colts' captain who scored to take a 4-3 lead.

No one was cheering now.

By the time the next ball was thrown in, Alfie was starting to feel a little bit better. Although he still hadn't recovered quite enough to get to the ball first, he was able to stop Jasper from getting a clear shot at goal, and eventually managed to force him backwards until Jasper had no option but to put the ball out for a throw-in quite close to his own goal.

Thinking fast, Alfie rushed to the ball

as quickly as he could given his bruised and battered condition, and nudged it in front of him with his right foot before taking a shot with his left. Because the pitch was by now so muddy it seemed to take the ball ages to cross the goal line, but eventually it did just that, despite Jasper's best efforts to stop the ball from doing so.

Alfie threw his hands aloft and turned to face the crowd who had started cheering again.

What he and the crowd hadn't noticed, however, and what Jasper had, was that Keith had not actually blown his whistle to give the goal. So while Alfie was busy celebrating, Jasper had taken the ball past him and scored in Alfie's goal.

Keith's whistle sounded. "Goal. 5-3 to Jasper, and that's half-time."

"What!" cried Alfie and the crowd, seemingly all at once. "That was my goal," Alfie stated.

"No it wasn't. The whole ball didn't cross the line," replied Keith smiling. "You should play to the whistle, Jones. Did old man Grimshaw not teach you anything when he was coach?"

Despite all the protests, Keith stuck by his decision and eventually Alfie and his supporters had to accept that he was 5-3 down and facing an uphill battle to save the future of the Colts.

Chapter twenty

Jimmy Grimshaw was grinning from ear-to-ear as Alfie made his way over to him during the half-time break.

Alfie, though, looked far from happy. He was covered from head-to-toe in mud, breathing heavily and holding his chest, which was still feeling extremely sore following his earlier encounter with Jasper.

"Why are you smiling?" Alfie just about managed to ask the old man in-between taking deep breaths. "I'm losing."

"Maybe so, but you're definitely going to win," Jimmy answered confidently.

"How do you know?" Alfie enquired. Just

then an equally big smile spread across the small boy's face as well. "Are you going to cheat, too?" he asked hopefully.

At first Jimmy looked a little disappointed by what Alfie had just asked him, but the big smile quickly reappeared on his face and he began to chuckle. "Oh, Alfie don't be so silly," said the old coach merrily. "There's really no need for me to cheat in order for you to win. I only need to be fair. The three times that Keith played a fair point just then you scored every time. Keep trying your hardest and you'll be fine."

But Alfie still wasn't so sure. "But my chest hurts really, really badly," he whined. "So do my legs. I really don't think I can carry on."

Jimmy was just about to reassure Alfie that he would be alright, when Billy came running over to see his friend.

"That was sooo unfair, Alf. You're playing so much better than Jasper. Are you okay? That foul he did on you was well out of order."

Alfie looked at Jimmy and then at Billy. Both his best friend and his old coach were obviously very concerned by the pain he was so clearly in, and although Alfie really did feel like quitting, at the same time he didn't want to let his friends down.

"I'll be fine," he eventually replied, not really sounding as though he meant it.

"That's good," Billy continued. "We're all cheering for you. Even that weird old lady wants you to win."

Alfie's ears suddenly pricked up. "What weird old lady?"

"That one over there," replied Billy, vaguely waving his left hand in the direction he had just run from. "That one standing just... oh, she's gone. Never mind. She wanted you to win anyway."

"What did she look like?"

"Just... like an old lady I guess," answered Billy. "I can't really remember. I don't even know who she is. She just asked me what the score was, I told her and then she said she hoped you'd win. That's it."

"Can't you remember anything else about her?" Alfie pleaded. "Please Billy, try. It's important."

Billy looked more than a little confused by his best friend's sudden interest in the old woman, but sensing it was, for some reason, really important to Alfie, he tried to remember something else. "Well... about the only other thing is that she had a green and purple dress on and was wearing a silly old purple tea towel on her head. It looked really stupid. Oh, and she said something about a magic bear, but I don't know what she was talking about. I heard Chloe's Mum tell my Dad that she was probably mad."

Alfie smiled. He knew that the old lady most certainly wasn't mad. He also now knew that he would definitely beat Jasper.

Madam Zola was back.

Chapter twenty one

Within moments of the second half starting, Alfie scored a goal to reduce Jasper's lead to just one.

He had now all but forgotten about the pain he had been feeling at the end of the first half. When Jimmy threw the ball in for the second time it was once again Alfie who got control of it. Seconds later he had levelled the score at 5-5.

The watching boys were now cheering on their friend at the top of their voices, while even some of the parents had started joining in the chanting of Alfie's name.

This crowd support made Alfie feel

really good inside and he became increasingly more confident with every encouraging shout that he heard from the sideline.

He scored the next two goals to move into a 7-5 lead. Both goals came as the result of a fine piece of skill that he wouldn't have felt comfortable trying just ten minutes earlier.

Jasper could not believe what was happening. Both he and Keith had been shocked when Alfie had wanted to continue the game given the obvious pain the smaller boy had been in at the end of the first-half. "He won't be back," Keith had said, putting an arm proudly around his son's broad shoulders during the half-time break. "Football's as much about strength and power as it is skill and speed and that little squirt just hasn't got enough."

Watching Alfie now running rings around his son, Keith thought back to those very words.

If Jasper was going to go on and win this game he would have to put his obvious size advantage to good use. "Stop the game," Keith shouted to Jimmy, just as Alfie had scored his eighth goal, leaving Jasper sprawled on the floor looking dazed and confused in the process.

"Why?" asked Jimmy.

"Jasper needs his shoelaces tied," Keith lied.

Although this was clearly a fib, Keith was already on the pitch and talking to his son, while making a not at all convincing show of pretending to tie Jasper's shoelaces, before Jimmy could either accept or refuse the request.

Alfie watched the father and son talking to each other. He had fully expected Keith and Jasper to have one more trick in store, so he wasn't at all surprised when he saw that familiar unpleasant smile pass between both of their lips.

This time, though, he wasn't scared. Alfie was still fully confident that he was going to win – especially as he only needed two more goals and Jasper required five.

After Keith had finally made his way off the pitch, making a big show of saying sorry to Jimmy, Alfie and the crowd for holding up play, the game restarted.

As had been the case throughout the second-half, Alfie reached the ball first and used his skill to get past Jasper with ease, bamboozling his opponent with two step-overs and tricking the larger boy into going one way while he went the other.

Alfie sprinted away from his nemesis, using his superior speed to leave Jasper trailing in his wake. But whereas before, Jasper, realising that he wouldn't catch Alfie, had simply given up the chase, this time he had continued to keep on running – even after Alfie had side footed the ball into the empty goal to go 9-5 in front. In fact, the Colt's captain didn't stop running until he had barged into Alfie's back at full speed, sending the unsuspecting boy flying through the goal to join the ball.

"Sorry," shouted Jasper straight away. "The ground was too wet and I just couldn't stop myself from running. Good goal Alfie, you're just too fast for me. No hard feelings?"

Nobody for one second believed Jasper's apology. After all, it's hard to believe that someone is really sorry when they can't stop themselves from grinning while saying that they didn't really mean to do something.

But then nobody was really taking much notice of Jasper anyway. Everyone, apart from Keith and his son, had rushed over to check that Alfie, who for the second time that morning was lying prone in the mud, was okay.

"Give him some space," ordered Jimmy, while pouring some water onto the back of Alfie's head. The young boy grunted as the cold liquid splashed onto his neck.

"Can you hear me, Alfie?" Jimmy said loudly into his ear, being careful not to move the boy just in case he was badly hurt.

"Un-huh," muttered Alfie after a few seconds.

"Take your time, son," said Jimmy gently, as Alfie tried to turn from his front onto his back.

"How many fingers am I holding up," the old man asked once Alfie had managed to wearily sit himself up.

"Three," Alfie replied, correctly. "What happened? It feels like I've been run over by a steamroller."

Jimmy laughed. "You may as well have been the way Jasper ran into you then."

At that moment Keith walked over to them. "Sorry about that, Alfie. It was a total accident. Jasper just couldn't stop running. He feels so bad about what happened."

Keith tried to keep the smile off his face

as he apologised but, like Jasper, he just couldn't do it. "So what happens now?" Keith continued.

"What do you mean what happens now," snapped Jimmy, trying his best not to get angry. "It's obvious that Alfie can't continue after that... that... tackle, if you can call it a tackle."

"Are you trying to suggest my son would do something like that on purpose?" Keith asked in what he hoped was an innocent tone. "I've already told you it was an accident," he smirked wickedly.

Jimmy said nothing and when some of the parents moved forward to confront Keith, the old man held his hand up to stop them.

"So I guess that means I... sorry, I mean Jasper... wins, seeing as poor little Alfie can't possibly complete the game."

Jimmy felt as if he was going to explode with rage. He simply couldn't believe that all Keith was worried about was winning the challenge when a young boy was so obviously badly hurt.

The old man was just about to finally lose his temper with Keith when he was stopped in his tracks by a small voice.

"Who says I quit?" Alfie had struggled to his feet, and despite swaying a little from side to side, he didn't actually look too badly hurt.

"There's no way I can let you continue, Alfie," said Jimmy sorrowfully. "You may have a concussion. I'm sorry"

"Then we win," Keith barked triumphantly. "Come on Jasper let's go home."

"Please Jimmy," Alfie pleaded. "I'm okay, I promise."

Jimmy looked at Alfie. He really did not want the young boy to continue, but he could see by the look on his face just how much playing on meant to him.

"Well... okay, but if I think you're getting any worse then I'm calling an end to it – win or lose? Fair."

Alfie nodded and began to make his way back to his goal line. He could hardly walk and to Jimmy it looked as though every step the young boy took was an almighty effort.

Keith and Jasper were once again shocked by the small boy's resilience, but seeing as how their adversary could now hardly walk, they were not at all concerned that Alfie had chosen to play on – in spite of the fact Jasper was losing by four goals.

***

Unsurprisingly, the next time Jimmy threw the ball into play, it was Jasper who got to it first. Although Alfie tried the best he possibly could to tackle his opponent, he no longer had enough strength left to compete adequately. Jasper shrugged off Alfie's challenge as easily as you would swat a fly and kicked the ball as hard as he could into the goal. 9-6.

The next goal came in much the same way, with Jasper once again taking full advantage of his injured rival to score. At 9-7 the game was very much in the balance.

The crowd had now gone almost totally silent again. Everyone watching feared the worst. They couldn't possibly see how Alfie could win when he could hardly walk, let alone run. Within seconds, the crowd's fears grew even greater as Jasper again beat Alfie to the ball and then brushed past him to score and reduce their friend's lead to just a single goal.

Now there was only one person cheering. "Come on Jasper," roared a delighted Keith. "Show them how a real footballer does it."

Jasper smiled at his Dad and gave him the thumbs up. He was about to reply to

Keith when he saw something that really surprised him.

Alfie was smiling.

Despite the fact he could hardly walk, and seemingly had no chance of winning the game, Alfie was actually grinning from ear to ear. In fact, he was almost laughing.

"What are you so happy about, muppet?" Jasper asked him, trying not to sound too surprised by his opponent's seemingly good mood. "You've got no chance of winning this game. There's no way you can possibly beat me now."

"Maybe not," agreed Alfie, who was still smiling and sounded remarkably happy. "So why don't you do what your Dad says and show us all how a real footballer does it?"

"What do you mean?"

"I bet you can't score a goal from a really long way out like a real professional player could."

Now it was Jasper's turn to laugh. "Don't be so silly, of course I can. I've got the hardest shot in school. You just wait and see muppet. I'll show you."

Once both players had got back to their lines, Jimmy threw the ball into the middle. It was Jasper, of course, who reached the ball first. However, instead of getting the ball and going as close as he could to Alfie's goal before taking his shot, as he had been doing up to now, he decided to try something different.

"Watch this, Dad," Jasper shouted, as he attempted – and failed – to flick the ball off the floor with his right foot.

"Jasper, what are you doing?" Keith shouted back, sounding concerned.

His son didn't reply. He was still trying to flick the ball into the air. On the fourth attempt he managed it. Then, while the ball was still in the air he swung his boot at it as hard as he could.

The sound of the thud as Jasper's boot connected with the ball was ear-achingly loud.

Even by Jasper's standards this was a powerful kick. Possibly the most powerful kick he had ever managed.

There was just one problem. As usual, Jasper had been more worried about getting power into the ball than he had been about where the ball was actually going to go. So while Jasper looked hopefully towards Alfie's goal, hoping to see the ball land between the two traffic cones that marked it out, Alfie, and everyone watching, had their eyes fixed

157

firmly on Jasper's goal – where the ball was actually heading.

Instead of kicking the ball forward, Jasper had managed to miss-kick it horribly and sent the ball flying over his own head. When he finally realised what he had done he turned round just in time to see the ball cross his own goal line.

Against all odds Alfie had won. Jasper and Keith would have to leave the Colts.

All of the watching Colt's players, led by Billy, charged towards Alfie as fast as they could, cheering at the top of their voices as they ran.

They lifted their friend high above

their heads and carried him off the pitch, where he received a hero's welcome from the watching parents.

Jimmy, meanwhile, went to shake hands with Keith. But the now former coach was already storming off in the direction of his car, quickly followed by an apologising, and rather embarrassed looking, Jasper.

Chapter twenty two

On Christmas Eve, Alfie was standing with his Dad and Megan outside another Santa's Grotto.

Alfie's sister had decided that she wanted to see Santa one more time before Christmas, just to be sure he definitely knew what she wanted. Mr Jones had agreed to take her to the Grotto in town to see him.

As the three of them stood patiently in a long queue in the middle of Kingsway's indoor shopping centre, Alfie suddenly noticed a shop he couldn't remember ever having seen before.

"Is it alright if I go in there for a

minute, Dad? I promise I'll be back out before Meg goes into see Santa."

"I suppose that's alright Alfie. But why on earth do you want to go in a shop that sells wind chimes?"

But Alfie didn't reply. He was too busy running towards the shop.

Once he got there he wasn't at all surprised to see that the shop was completely empty. He made his way slowly to the counter. "Hello," he shouted at the top of his voice. "Is there anybody there?"

Within seconds he heard the wind chimes start to chime as someone entered the shop. "Looking for someone?" asked a familiar voice from behind.

Alfie turned and smiled. "I thought this must be your shop," he said excitedly.

"This isn't my shop," Madam Zola replied. She was dressed exactly the same way as she had been when Alfie had first met her at the funfair. "I'm a customer. Just like you are. Why else would I have come through the front door?"

Alfie didn't know whether to believe her. He didn't really care if it was her shop or not. He was just glad to see her.

"I just wanted to say thanks," he said after a short pause.

161

"That's nice," answered Madam Zola, sounding confused. "Thanks for what?"

"For getting Jimmy to come back as coach of the Colts and then helping me to beat Jasper."

Madam Zola chuckled. "Who's Jimmy? I don't know anyone called Jimmy," she replied. "I didn't help you beat Jasper. You beat him by yourself. I heard you played very well."

"You were there watching, weren't you?"

The fortune teller thought to herself for a moment "I... I... I'm an old woman Alfie. You can't expect me to remember everywhere I've been in the last week or so."

Alfie shook his head, smiling as he did so. "Anyway, thanks to you I can continue playing for the Colts."

"Which means your destiny to be a professional footballer is still very much alive, Alfie. Well done. Let's hope you fulfil your dream."

"What else will I need to do?" Alfie asked, although he knew the fortune teller wouldn't tell him anything. Not yet anyway.

"Time will tell," she said, much as he had expected. "Anyway you had better go. I can hear your Dad calling you."

Sure enough, Alfie too could hear his Dad shouting his name. "Megan must be next to go in," he said to himself. "Well, thanks for everything Madam Zola, I know you helped really, even if you say you didn't."

He made his way to the shop door and opened it. "Will I ever see you again?" he asked, but when he turned around to hear Madam Zola's answer he found himself staring at an empty shop.

When Alfie got back to his Dad he discovered that the reason his father had called his name wasn't because Megan was next in line to see Santa. It was because he was standing talking to Billy and Mr Morris, who were in town doing some last minute Christmas shopping.

"Hey, Alf have you heard the news?" Billy called over as soon as he saw Alfie approaching.

"No. What's up?"

"Keith's starting up a new team and he's going to make sure they play the Colts. Jasper will be really out to get you if we do play them. You'll have to be well careful."

Alfie just smiled. He'd be alright.

Madam Zola would make sure of that.

Turn the page to read the opening chapter of **Split Loyalties** *- a Kindle only book written by David Fuller.*

Download your copy today...

Hugh

Hugh Capulet had been completely obsessed with football for as long as he – or anyone else for that matter – could remember.

From the very moment that Hugh had taken his first unsteady steps at just over ten-months old, a ball had rarely been far from his feet.

As a baby, he would simply refuse point blank to fall asleep unless a football was placed in his cot, while few, if any, childhood photos of Hugh exist in which he's not either kicking or dribbling a ball.

In fact, there is probably more chance of seeing a photo of the Loch Ness Monster and Bigfoot sitting together whilst enjoying a quiet cup of tea on the lawns of Buckingham Palace, than there is of seeing a picture of an adolescent Hugh without a ball somewhere near his feet.

Given the extent of his obsession, it's probably not all that surprising to learn that Hugh began to exhibit a talent for the sport before he was even out of nappies. He was as comfortable dribbling a football as most babies are dribbling their dinner down their clothes.

By the age of nine, Hugh had been selected for League One Portland Town's Academy team. He signed his first professional contract with the same club on his seventeenth birthday, having won the team's player of the year award every single season since first joining the academy.

It didn't take long for Premier League scouts to recognise Hugh's obvious potential. Whilst still a teenager he signed his first multi-million pound contract with the newly-crowned league champions, Lexington Albion – England's most successful ever football team.

Since then, a raft of individual and team honours had come his way and he had even become a regular for the Italian national team.

Yet, in spite of all the trophies that he'd won, the fan adulation he'd received, and the massive amounts of money he had earned in the seven years since first signing for Lexington, it was still a love of football, rather than any other associated reward, that made him tick.

Each and every time he stepped onto a pitch, he still received the exact same buzz that he had experienced before playing his very first match as a six year old for the Ashgate Athletic under 7s.

His heart beat would start to race and a nervous shiver of excitement would run down the entire length of his spine. An involuntary beaming smile would then break out across his face.

For years he had tended to be the first player to arrive at Lexington's luxurious Middleton training complex every single day, and more often than not he would be the last to leave, too.

And when he wasn't playing in a match or at training, the chances were that he was either watching a match on the TV, or playing one of his many football-related console games.

Yes, it's fair to say that Hugh Capulet had been completely obsessed with football for a very, very long time.

Until now.

There was just one day remaining

before Hugh was due to meet up with his Italian teammates ahead of boarding a plane to travel to Brazil for the World Cup and Hugh should have been buzzing with excitement. This was due to be his first major international tournament, having picked up a tournament-ending knee injury on the eve of the European Championships two years earlier.

Feeling fit and healthy, and having just had the best season of his career with Lexington, he should have been looking forward to the prospect of playing in the biggest football tournament of all. He should have been as excited as a hyperactive four-year-old on Christmas Eve.

Instead he was dreading it.

And it was all his family's fault.

Visit the Kindle store today to read the rest of Split Loyalties